Gerait's Daughter

Gerait's Daughter

MILLIE J. RAGOSTA

DOUBLEDAY & COMPANY, INC.

GARDEN CITY, NEW YORK

1981

35990

Library of Congress Cataloging in Publication Data

Ragosta, Millie J
Gerait's daughter.

I. Title.
PS3568.A413G4   813'.54
ISBN: 0-385-17274-5
Library of Congress Catalog Card Number 80–2759

First Edition

for my father
in most loving remembrance

Gerait's Daughter

CHAPTER 1

High above the keep of Dublin Castle, a solitary gull, a bare shade darker than the restless, gray river below, soared downriver toward the sea. The skies, drooping watered silk, seemed to wait like the spectators along the quay for the arrival of the English ship which was battling the icy winds whipping around the guarding castle on the peninsula of Howth.

My father and I, surrounded by his small entourage, sat on horseback a little apart from the Dubliners, as befitted the Lord Deputy to the Viceroy of Ireland and his household. Or so we all hoped he still was. Perhaps the struggling English ship would carry an edict from King Henry to remove him from his post, for, even after the six years since Henry Tudor had taken the English crown from Richard III at Bosworth Field, my father had not entirely relinquished his Yorkist sympathies, to the displeasure of the Lancastrian king.

So we still called Henry Tudor even though he'd married Princess Elizabeth, the oldest daughter of the Yorkist, Edward IV, to end, once and for all, he said, the futile struggle between the houses of York and Lancaster. And, although my father, Gerald Fitzgerald, the eighth Earl of Kildare, had been a faithful adherent to the Yorkist Plantagenets, as had his family before him, the king had, cautiously and with various provisions, retained him to rule the Anglo-Irish within the Pale, or the counties surrounding Dublin. He declared he had so done in the interests of conciliation and peace; Mother's father, Roland FitzEustace, Baron Portlester, flatly declared it was because only

my father could keep the "wild" Irish beyond the Pale
from collecting black rent from the king himself. Though
Father's family had come to Ireland four hundred years
ago with the Conqueror, and he was, thus, technically
English, his family, the Geraldines, over the years had become more Irish than the Irish. Gerait More, or Great Gerald, they called him in the native Gaelic, and there was no
man in Ireland who commanded more respect.

When I'd been a little maid, I'd thought they called him
"more" from the great size of him and the magnificent look
of him, but my sister Eleanor, who's a year older than I,
laughed and said it was because he was chief of the Geraldines.

All eyes were upon him now. His horse was gray, gray
as the day, but everything else about him was fiery bright.
His blue eyes, his wiry reddish-brown hair, the long, curly
locks blowing forward to mingle with his luxuriant mustache, and his saffron-dyed shirt were indeed a sight to fill
Irish eyes. I watched him proudly, wondering if the English king would again attempt to forbid the wearing of
such "Irish" hair and garb as many another had done.
He'd tried without success so far to outlaw the speaking of
the Gaelic and the voicing of war cries of the clans.
"Croom-abo" was the Fitzgerald cry, which meant,
roughly, "our lands forever." Such cries incited the Irish to
wildness, the king had declared, and said if we must shout
when going into battle, let it be something like "For Saint
George and England" or "For Henry."

"It's just as easy to refuse to cry 'For Henry' as it was to
cry 'For Edward' or 'For Richard,'" my father'd said im-
perturbably when we'd first heard Henry had won at Bosworth, for, although he was a true adherent of the Yorkist
kings, his family loyalty took precedence in Ireland. "You
know, Milord Father, those silly damned rulings don't
mean a thing in Ireland," he'd continued, addressing
Grandfather FitzEustace.

I have heard it said that there is usually much dissension among intermarrying families, but never have I seen anything like that in our home. My father had been fast friend to Mother's father since he'd served under him in the Brotherhood of Saint George, the brigade that defended the Pale. And Grandfather FitzEustace had liked Father well enough to give him his only daughter to marry. Shortly after, when his wife had died, the old man had come to live with them, where he taught each of us, as we became old enough, Irish history the like of which no seanachie (historian) in the land could have done. And, though each was a quick-tempered, proud and fine-strung man, never did I hear anything but amiability between them.

Nevertheless, Grandfather had not entirely agreed with Father's sanguine assessment of the situation.

"I hope you're right, Gerald, but there are differences this time. This Henry Tudor is a usurper, after all. Despite his fantastic claims of being descended from Cadwallader and King Arthur and his bastardized descent from John of Gaunt, even in spite of marrying the Princess Elizabeth, he took the throne by force, and by force he'll have to keep it. He'll enforce his decrees against our 'Irishness.'"

"Be a damned fool to try," Father'd replied.

But Henry had tried. Indeed, there'd been one rebellion already when Father and half the Irish lords had backed a boy who claimed to be King Edward's nephew, the Earl of Warwick, in a vain bid for the throne. The king had put down the rebellion quickly and made a spit boy of the boy "king," who'd really been named Lambert Simnel. But not before the English Earl of Lincoln, another of King Edward's nephews, and my own Uncle Thomas Fitzgerald, along with many others, had been killed.

Now, as we awaited the English ship, Grandfather Fitz-Eustace frowned and bit his lip. He couldn't have been more different than my father, being straight and small and slender, with a thin, aristocratic nose and face and deep-set blue eyes.

"I fear, Gerald, that the king will have sent a good, staunch Lancastrian . . . perhaps Thomas Butler . . . to govern Ireland," he said.

"By Saint Bride, Milord Father, God forbid that he should ever appoint a *Butler* to rule in Ireland! Better the devil!"

"God knows he's not been too pleased with *you*, lad. I fear you may have to face it. Sir Thomas would be a logical choice."

"He'd never stay in Ireland," Father said with a contemptuous note in his voice. "He was ever an Anglophile to start with, and took the first ship to England when he heard the Tudor had won at Bosworth."

"They've passed the headland," interjected one of Father's younger kern, Jimmy Boyce, a blithe lad who larded his upper lip to encourage the growth of hair thereon and who dogged Father's footsteps everywhere.

I watched as the ship tacked against the wind, wondering if the long-dreaded demotion for Father would be brought by those aboard. At eighteen, I was finally allowed to accompany Father and the band of retainers who followed him everywhere without begging permission from the Lady Allison, my mother, who had never thought it seemly for a girl to want to ride abroad with the men.

Mother was pregnant again and hoped this time there'd be another son in case anything happened to four-year-old Gerry. Girls could not rule a clan, and so boys were important as tanists, heirs. They must also be perfect, since the Irish would never tolerate a maimed or imperfect man as leader. So important was this that when a tanist was captured in battle, like as not the wild Irish would put out an eye, lop off an ear, a hand, or something even more precious to the youth, to prevent him leading out the clan he sprang from.

There were four of us girls—Eleanor, also called Nell; me—Margaret; Alice and Elizabeth, who we called Beth. Eleanor was nearly nineteen, not even a full year older than I, and as big and strong as a man. She was also very beautiful, with a great sweetness in her direct, blue gaze. She stomped and yelled like Father, and, like him, had a heart as big as the courtyard at Maynooth, dragging home every stray, animal or human, in County Meath. Her eyes were the same royal blue of Grandfather FitzEustace, her hair as black and curling as Mother says his was before it had silvered. I loved her dearly; yet we two went at it hammer and tongs most of the time. Mother said putting us in the same room was tantamount to locking a Butler and a Fitzgerald in a horse stall together.

I was nearly as tall as Eleanor, but slender like Mother and Grandfather. And though Alice says it's unseemly of me to say so, it's my pride and good fortune that I look much like our mother too.

Her skin was delicate and white, seldom showing the bright pink mine does when I'm angry or laughing. Her face was exceedingly slender and high of cheek, and her eyes looked out on the world, gray as a dove's wing and gentle as its murmur. She seemed unaware of her great beauty entirely except for her hair, which was no small source of pride to her. It was as silky as the fine Flemish cloth Father occasionally bought us off ships in Waterford Harbor, and the exact color of chestnuts at their maturity. Scissors had never touched it, so that it hung well below her knees when she unbound it. Each Friday, she and her women washed it. Then, for half a day, she'd take her needlework and sit before the hall fire to dry it, or, on a fine summer day, on the sun-drenched drawbridge. Father grumbled that the castle lads, pages, squires and kern, not to mention the knights, who should know better, always managed to find work in the vicinity of Mother's hair-drying. We children said he knew that because there was he, foremost among them. He'd laugh and agree, calling Mother's hair the glory of Maynooth.

Which was no exaggeration. The mere sight of Mother's hair was enough to have made Strongbow's wife, Red Eva, gnash her beautiful teeth in envy. Our legends say she used to braid chunks of iron into her long red hair and

then use the braids as flails against her enemies. Mother
never braided anything more lethal than sprigs of lavender
or gillyflowers into hers, but she felled the greatest knight
in Ireland with them.

And, thanks be to God and Saint Bridget, mine was
likely to be as lovely when it had years enough to grow as
long as hers. I never would dare to say so aloud, since even
mild Beth said I was "full of myself," and Father declared
me quite conceited.

Beth looked like Father but had Mother's sweet nature
and expression. I was reversed, with Father's wild and ungovernable nature, impulsive, proud and rebellious, but I
had Mother's face and form. And often have I wondered,
if heaven had given me the choice of it, would I have pre-
ferred Beth's combination to my own? I longed to be gentle and good and beloved like Mother, but I noticed it was
always Father who got his own way. And it was very nice
to look like her. Men stared at me with the soft, specula-
tive expression Father wore when staring at Mother in the
firelight, just before bedtime. Many of the Anglo-Irish
barons had negotiated for my hand in behalf of their sons,
but our parents were in no hurry to bestow us, saying they
were content to allow us our own choice, if it were at all
suitable, as they had been.

Beth was thirteen, with an even disposition and cheery
manner that earned her no animosity from any of us,
which was the wonder of Ireland when you consider the
way things were between the other three of us. Alice was
only eight, but she kept the entire household in a continual
turmoil, stomping and shouting about like a miniature Father without the mustache. Once, indeed, when she'd been
very small and Father'd caught her making mead in his
best helmet by stirring a quantity of honey and hot water
therein, his outraged roar had scared and angered her to
the extent that she threw the entire mess right through the
newly installed painted window in the library. It had
depicted the rescue of the first Earl of Kildare from the
nursery of Woodstock Castle when fire broke out, by the

family's pet ape, which was the incident that had inspired the family arms. Father had sent all the way to England for the glazier who'd made the glorious thing, and all the lakes in Ireland would not have held his pride in it. Moreover, there was no ready money at the time to pay for a new one. It was a measure of his love that Father didn't kill Alice on the spot. Then there was our only lad, Gerry, who was four years old and the darling of the house. He was a FitzEustace in manner and appearance, scholarly and slight, with a gentle, winning way about him. If Father ever wished he'd been more robust, he certainly didn't say so. Gerry was the pride of his life and worthy to be tanist of Fitzgerald, small and wiry though he was.

However, despite all my meandering among the people I love, a habit I have never been able to break, I had ridden out with my father and his men when word had come to Saint Thomas Court, our Dublin residence due to Father's capacity as deputy, despite Mother's uncertainty that it was seemly. Since Father liked having me and I was quite safe with his troop, and since there was nothing in the world I liked better than riding a fine hobby, I sat and watched the ship lay to and its crew scamper across the deck, securing sails and putting the landing bridge into place.

There were several Englishmen aboard, waiting in various attitudes to disembark. Two of them, obviously the ranking ones, stepped forward onto the small set of steps as soon as they were fairly in place. The foremost of the two was a powerfully built man, dark of visage and eye, what we Irish called a "black Irishman." He was clean-shaven in the English fashion, his apparel English too, magnificent black doublet and hose with a crimson cloak thrown over. The cloak was unfastened, the better to show his splendid clothes, and flapped foppishly in the brisk October wind. He was, perhaps, twenty-five and handsome. He glanced up at my father's standard, flying proudly from Lionel Howth's hand, a cynical smile curling his lips.

Behind him, the second, somewhat younger, man stood

quietly surveying the dockside and its occupants. He was dressed more quietly in gray wool, his cloak lined with "bogy" or lambswool, although he sensibly held it shut with one hand so that only a small tail whipping in the stiff wind showed its lining. He bore a faint resemblance to the other man, although his eyes were a soft brown rather than the obsidian black of his companion. His quiet appearance, however, was set at variance by the startling red of his hair. It stood out against the weathered-white ship timbers like the Beltane fire the country folk still light to ward off evil on May Day Eve.

"By Jesus Christ and all His Saints, the king has sent us a plague of Butlers—Black James, the bastard, and his bookish cousin, Sir Piers," Father exploded.

"Father, Mother told you to curb your tongue," I said self-righteously, staring curiously at the two Butlers.

"Damn it, Magheen, I'm not calling him a name; he *is* a bastard. His father, Sir John, who was the sixth Earl of Ormonde, never married. He got this black whelp on wild Reynolda O'Brien. So, being illegitimate, he can't inherit the title. His Uncle Thomas Butler was given it . . ." He broke off and threw me a sharp look. "Never mind. You watch your pointed little tongue or I'll be scooting you back to your mother's side, where a maidenly lass would be anyhow."

Undaunted, I smiled impudently, for I knew he liked my company and wouldn't enforce any of his frequent threats of discipline. Already his attention had returned to the newcomers.

Sir James, the one Father had called bastard, beamed maliciously at Father.

"Ah, Kildare, I've been hoping with all my heart you'd be here when I landed," he said resonantly.

"Then, by Saint Bride, it must be tidings likely to discomfort me that you're carrying," was the grim reply. He stared down at the two men from the eminence of his great hobby. "James the black and Piers the red. Butlers like a pair of French playing cards. And one of you at least is a knave."

The younger man met Father's gaze unflinchingly—indeed, almost insolently—a slight, amused smile flickering across his full lips. He extended a hand in a straightforward way, and, after a pause, Father took it.

"God's greeting, milord. My uncle, Sir Thomas Butler, bids me convey his greetings to you as well," he said with quiet confidence.

"When you see your uncle next, you may convey mine to him, Sir Piers," Father said with grudging respect. Then, characteristically, being more than willing to give credit where it was due, he added, "There's nothing wrong with you and your uncle, short of being Butlers, which, God knows, you can't help. It was your good fortune that Sir Thomas had the rearing of you after your parents' deaths."

Sir James laughed unpleasantly. "And that tone seems to imply *I'd* have been better off after mine died had I been placed with Sir Thomas instead of my O'Brien kin."

"I'm not condemning the O'Briens, Sir James," Father answered evenly, "but you might just mention to them when you meet that I'll not tolerate them trying to collect black rent from the people of Meath any more than I did the O'Rileys."

Sir James frowned.

"I've no desire to stand here in the cold discussing the supposed depredations of those you're expected to control and govern. Especially since I've king's business to discuss with you when we reach Saint Thomas Court. Have you a lad or two to help with our baggage?"

Father nodded curtly to Lionel Howth and Jimmy Boyce, who dismounted to help the Butlers' people.

"You can mount their horses," Father said grudgingly. "Hospitality demands that anyone who seeks the shelter of my roof must be served."

Sir James mounted with elaborate grace, and in the doing his gaze fell on me.

"Ho, Kildare, from the set of the maid's jaw and the scornful expression of her, I'd know her for your daughter. But her looks are those of the luscious Lady Allison. A tasty wench, indeed."

"Mind your damned black tongue," Father roared, "or I'll pull it out of your mouth and jam it in your ear if your Saxon king hangs me for it."

He whirled his mount and forced it in between mine and Sir James's, grabbing my bridle to hurry me along. I threw the black Butler a murderous glance, not liking his light way of speaking about my mother or, for that matter, of myself. As we rode toward Newe Gate Street, I caught a glimpse of Sir Piers's wry amusement at the exchange. We rode the short distance home in a strained silence.

Baths had already been prepared for the newcomers when word had come from the harbor of their arrival, as was our custom. Mother and Walter Delahide, our steward, were busy directing the placing of trestle and forms in the great hall. She summoned pages to divest them of their cloaks, and told them dinner would await them when they'd bathed in the quarters already prepared for them.

When they'd retired, Father motioned his harper to play, which was always the first thing he thought of when he was perturbed. He began pacing back and forth in unconscious time to the music.

"By Saint Bride, lady," he muttered, leaning over to kiss my mother as he passed her, "the damned black Butler is enjoying my discomposure." He muttered some more words that made Mother frown and stalked off toward the chimney to forestall her objection. The harper, Sean McArdle, fixed his small, homely face in a rapt expression, his shrewd eyes gauging Father's face, and plucked with powerful fingers at the instrument he cradled, evoking the strains of a song composed, so our seanachies say, by Brian Boru's harper on the eve of the day the great hero destroyed Waterford.

My sister Eleanor came into the hall, elegant in her

English-style dress and took a stance near me at the edge of the family dais.

"*I* wouldn't climb the stairs to dress for the damned worthless Butlers," I hissed.

"Butlers, is it?" she cried. "Well, for once I agree with you. Had I known it was them, I'd not have changed either. But all the same, miss, you'd best not let Mother hear you swearing."

I sniffed but disdained to argue with her; I was more interested in watching my parents' reaction to the idea of Butlers at Saint Thomas Court.

Shortly, they and their people reappeared in the doorway. When Sean caught sight of them, he left off playing with an angry thwang and folded his arms, much to Sir Piers's amusement. Mother, always tactful, motioned to her own favorite bard, who, lute in hand, came forward to play softly as we ate, in the manner Mother favored.

"Hurry and sit down, Nell," I whispered. "The quicker we eat, the quicker we hear what's going on in England and whether Father's in trouble again."

Our chaplain, Brother Joseph, must have had the same thought, for never did I hear bread so precipitously blessed.

Walter took the meats from the carver and handed huge trays to the kitchen boys for distribution about the hall. Mother motioned Sir James to a place at the family table along with his cousin. It had been necessary to put places on both sides of the table to accommodate the guests, so that we sat eyeing each other warily as we ate, with the exception of Mother, who tried to put everyone at ease, keeping the conversation general and uncontroversial. As soon as the courses had been placed, Walter sat down with us, obviously intent on hearing what the English visitors had to say, and arising only to direct the changing of the dishes.

By the time the seemingly interminable meal was finished, Father's impatience was boundless and evident.

This seemed to amuse Sir James; he lifted his cup to Walter to have it refilled, in no hurry to impart the news from England.

But now that all were fed, Mother pushed away her own trencher and cup and reached for her needlework. It was a tapestry for which I'd drawn the pattern. She looked expectantly at the visitors.

"We are anxious, now that you have eaten, to hear news of England," she hinted gently.

"Of course, dear Lady Allison." The dark face split in a fox-like grin. "There is news of interest to your husband."

"Out with it, then," Father said flatly, folding his big arms across his chest and trying to appear nonchalant.

Sir James lifted his cup in a sort of mocking salute.

"I'm sure the matter of greatest concern to you is whether or not His Highness has finally dealt with you as you deserve and removed you as deputy," he drawled.

Father's face was a study, scowling and barely contained.

"And has he?" Walter Delahide burst out impetuously.

"Not yet, Sir Walter, not yet."

Father's relief was manifest but he barely grunted.

Sir Walter, however, grinned broadly. "At least he's wise enough to know there is none other than Gerait More who can rule Ireland," he said with satisfaction.

Sir James made a sour face but contented himself with a negligent flick of his hand.

"Well, then, you damned Lancastrian clown, why are you wearing that damned fox-in-the-henhouse air?" Father barked.

"My lord of Kildare," Sir Piers interjected, "I hope you can find it in your heart to stop using terms like 'Lancastrian' and 'Yorkist' now. Hasn't the king showed how earnestly he desires such partisanship laid to rest by marrying the Princess Elizabeth? Why, he has even devised a pink Tudor rose as his house's badge to show the joining of the white rose of York and the red rose of Lancaster. The two houses now share England's throne."

My father threw Piers a grudging grin.

"He showed good sense in that, at least. Since Edward's sons went into the Tower when their Uncle Richard was Protector and have not emerged nor been seen again, it's only right that his daughter should be his heiress to the throne, one way or t'other."

Sir James seemed a little taken aback at Father's attitude.

"Aye," Walter said with a touch of indignation. "He took good care to tie up every string anyone might ever be tempted to unravel by marrying Princess Bess. If there were those who didn't quite believe in his descent from King Arthur and Cadwallader or that his ancestor's bastardy was not undone by royal decree, why he could always say he was king because his wife was queen."

"The king wishes all factions to be forgotten now," Piers said sharply. "Too long England has been torn between these warring families . . . like a well-chewed bone between two mastiffs. And he's been wonderfully forebearing toward you, milord, even when you aided and abetted . . . even crowned the organ-maker's son. It seems to me you'd do well to accept his hand in friendship."

"I don't need a Butler to tell me what I should do," Father said. He was silent for a long moment. "Still, you may tell the king I am honored by his confidence and, since Ireland has always been my foremost concern, I will serve him as well as I can. Now, so far as I can tell, you have no news that seriously disturbs me, Black James. What, then, is the meaning of that weasel smirk?"

Sir James's eyes flashed brilliantly, and the amused quirk again appeared at the corner of his mouth.

"In time. I must tell you also that my cousin, Piers, as you probably know, is now confirmed as heir to our Uncle Thomas. He will manage and control the Ormonde lands in Ireland. Of course, had I been . . . born otherwise . . . the title would be mine and not my Uncle Thomas's," he finished with a smile that didn't quite hide the bitter snarl in his eyes.

"Congratulations, Piers Roe," Father said. "I've no doubt you'll do a good job for your Uncle Thomas. Even as a little lad I remember you to have had a level head." He stared across the table at the younger man, his lips twitching as if to control a smile. "I remember something else too. Weren't you the little red-headed page to the Viscountess Barry when she visited Maynooth long ago? I recall getting up to go to early Mass and thrusting my feet into boots filled with warm oatmeal. And when I arrived late and barefoot to Mass, there was a little knave with a thatch like a puree of carrots watching me with the sharp, laughing eyes of a gnome."

Eleanor snickered and poked me in the ribs. We exchanged a look that deliciously shared the thought of Father's face when he felt the oatmeal. I looked at the Butler with new eyes. He had a fine, devious, original mind for the tricks that had delighted Nell, Alice and me all our lives.

"Will you accept the apologies of my maturity?" Sir Piers was saying. He didn't look the least bit sorry. Indeed, he seemed to be taking smug pleasure in the remembrance.

The tension in the hall had relaxed a little as Father recounted the prank. Almost as if he disliked seeing amity between Father and Piers, Sir James spoke up harshly.

"The resolving of ancient grievances and feuds is foremost in His Highness' mind and brings me to the reason I volunteered for this mission to Ireland."

Father's smile turned to a frown. He crossed his arms again with the air of saying, "Ah, we come to it at last."

"The king desires all his subjects to unite in Christian love and forgiveness," Sir James drawled.

"I would say, by his marrying the Princess and exacting no harsh penalties of those who opposed him at Bosworth, he's given us a fairly good example to follow," Mother said mildly, rethreading her needle.

Father nodded grudgingly.

"I'm glad to see you agree, Kildare," Sir James cried

gleefully. "Wouldn't you say, then, that his command that we Butlers and Fitzgeralds abandon forever our ancient strife is not unreasonable?"

Father stared at him with dawning suspicion, but under Mother's gentle, yet commanding stare he reddened and grunted assent.

"Good. Then you'll be entirely amenable to His Highness' plan for healing the breech once and for all. He bids you follow his example. He commands that Sir Piers marry one of your daughters."

For an infinitesimal moment, everyone in the hall drew a communal gasp. Nell clapped her hand over her mouth as if she, alone, had been responsible for the shocked sound.

Like a shot let loose from a sling, my father came out of his chair.

"By the Holy Beard of Christ," he exploded, "he wants to unite the blood of my daughter with a *Butler's?*"

"Aye, Kildare, aye," Sir James crowed. The black eyes of him snapped in delight.

I was on my feet too, glaring at him with a fury that nearly matched our sire's. Marry our Nelly to Piers Roe? For, of course, she being the oldest would be first chosen, as was the custom. I gritted my teeth and stared at them with loathing. Sir James was transported with joy, but, I had to admit, Sir Piers stared at his cousin distastefully and seemed embarrassed, almost apologetic.

To my astonishment, Mother smiled and reached out to touch his hand, her smile reassuring. What could she be thinking of, offering him this tacit sign of approval? It was akin to pulling the Fitzgerald banner off the wall and wiping up the floor spills with it.

"By Saint Bridget, never, never, never," Father roared.

"Get it out of your system, Kildare. Throw a trencher, why don't you? Shout and yell and make your rafters roar, you great ape of Kildare. And then, as you know you must, kneel down and obey the Crown."

Father glared at him balefully, murderously. His big

hands flexed as if he'd like to place them around his enemy's neck. He stared in stricken silence at Mother, who arose awkwardly and put her arms around him as far as her girth would allow, unmindful of the spectators.

"Don't, don't, darling," she crooned. "Perhaps . . . it's really for the best, you know. No, no, don't glare so, Gerald, think of it. The king is right."

He seemed to grow a bit calmer under her attentions and finally turned to gaze down at Sir Piers, who returned the stare with a certain sympathy.

"I am sorry, Milord Kildare, that my cousin has baited you so. I well knew how you'd take it and so have insisted upon coming with him to tell you." He threw his cousin a withering glance that held a trace of the abhorrence visible on the Fitzgerald faces. "Believe me, I had nothing to do with influencing the king's command. For, command it is. But I swear to you, I will treat your daughter with all the respect and honor due a daughter of Gerait More. One day your daughter will be Countess of Ormonde. And by this marriage the rivalry between our houses, which is so ancient no one can give a truly logical reason for it, will be at an end entirely."

I took Nell's cold hand in mine. "He's a well-spoken lad, Nelly, and comely enough too," I whispered resignedly. "You could do worse. Think of the Clanricarde Burkes with their belches and . . ."

"Shut up, you little traitor," she hissed, slapping at my hand and pulling her other free of mine. "*I'll* not be marrying him."

I subsided, pitying her, knowing she'd have to whether she would or no, and ashamed of my relief that it would be her instead of me. Yet, what I'd said was true enough. He *was* comely with eyes like a young roebuck, gentle, yet flashing fire, feeling his own powers. He spoke like a gentleman too, and, had he not been a Butler, I might even have liked him, I thought.

But, from our cradles we'd learned to distrust all Butlers, and, in spite of my ineffectual attempt to comfort my sister, my Mother's smile of approval seemed to me a betrayal of all the Geraldines.

"Well spoken, Sir Piers," she was saying staunchly. "And I, for one, applaud the king's wisdom. For how many years have our finest young men died on bloody fields over stupid clannishness."

She seized Father's hand and lifted it to her lips, forcing him to meet her eyes. What he saw there softened and encouraged him to do what he had no choice but to do. He smiled stiffly and reached out to shake Sir Piers's hand.

"Then, I'll be marrying my daughter Margaret to you," he said resignedly.

"What!" I cried. "But Eleanor's the oldest, Father."

Eleanor pinched my arm viciously. "Oh, you're a lovely sister," she snapped, "'*I* should not be upset,' you said. 'He's a comely lad and well-spoken,' you said. When you thought *I* would have to marry him. But you didn't know that Father agreed to betroth me to Calvagh O'Connor Faly only last week. The agreement's been signed."

"We'd planned to have the ceremony this Michaelmas, Magheen," Father said apologetically. "Eleanor didn't want you other girls to know until then."

Stung by Eleanor's secrecy—why, after all, had she kept such an important matter from me?—and furious that she'd told the entire hall I hadn't found the Butler obnoxious, I leaped to my feet wildly.

"It isn't fair; it isn't fair," I cried.

"Not fair, is it? You didn't mind throwing *me* to the Butler," Eleanor taunted.

Sir Piers was watching me with ill-concealed delight.

"I'm well-pleased, Milord Kildare," he said smoothly. "I had an opportunity to admire Lady Margaret as we rode to your palace, and she'll suit me well."

I flushed angrily. "I'll not marry you," I shouted, hearing my voice ululating like a wild Irishman's charging his enemy. "I have heard you say, Father, that a Butler is an abomination second only to a serpent, which, praise to God, Saint Patrick drove from Ireland long ago, and a pity he'd not the foresight to drive the Butlers with them. And now you're expecting me to marry one of them!"

Sir Piers's eyes were snapping with laughter.

"I won't marry you. I swear by Saint Bride, I won't," I cried. "I'll go Irish first."

"Shut up, Magheen!"

Father could still outshout me by a good deal, having the better of me in lung and throat size. "You will marry him! We must show the king our goodwill . . ."

"You'd marry me to a Butler just to show your goodwill?" I shrieked. "Indeed, Father, you've always made such a great fuss about being a kind and just father."

"Madam, what kind of impertinence do you countenance in your children?" Father cried, turning toward Mother.

"Aye, and that's another thing you do. We're always 'her children' when we're less than pleasing to you. You claim us readily enough when we do that which brings pride to the name of Fitzgerald, though. And so, it's entirely beyond me why you're not calling me 'your' child now. I'm the only Fitzgerald, it seems, mindful enough of our honor to protest this vile idea," I spat, too angry for caution.

"By the Holy Wimple of Saint Bride, I'll give you the beating I've been promising you since you were in infant's napkins," he thundered back, his blue eyes nearly popping from his head. "And then you'll marry him as I command."

"When frogs fly over Ireland, I'll marry him. The curse of Ronan Grantley upon you, James the Black and Piers the Red!"

I stomped down off the dais and began pacing the hall angrily.

"Magheen, my darling, you must gain control of yourself," Mother said mildly, her eyes full of pain at my display of temper. "Don't you realize what an honor it is to be the instrument for ending this useless enmity?"

I subsided a little. Taking my silence for the beginning of acceptance, she continued.

"Scripture says, 'Blessed are the peacemakers . . .'"

"'Peacemakers,' hell!" I burst out. "I'll give a Butler precious little peace, I can tell you."

"Stop that swearing in front of your mother," Father shouted, bringing his clenched fist down with a thump on her piled needlework. Howling in pain, he thrust his knuckles into his mouth for a moment, and then snatched them out, swearing.

Sir James was enjoying our distraction entirely.

"I want one thing," Father snapped, rounding on him. "And that's to see the last of you in my hall."

"Nay, I'm sorry to disappoint you, I'm to stay tonight and be prepared to take a letter stating your agreement back to His Highness in the morning. I'm sure you'll be happy to write it."

Mother smiled her acquiescence, and Father, although his face was thunderous, nodded reluctantly.

"You don't mean it," I wailed. "Never did I think the sun would rise on the day my own parents would sell me to a Butler to gain a Lancastrian king's goodwill."

"Shut up, Magheen, this doesn't concern you," Father yelled.

"Doesn't concern me? By the rood, Father, that's the stupidest thing ever I have heard you say. Mother's put up with your making plans for her without even consulting her all her life; I won't. I'll sign on as a gallowglass with the O'Hanlon. Yes, I will. I'll . . . . I'll cut my hair so they'll think me a lad . . ."

"Ah, Lady Margaret, that would be a shame to God," Sir Piers broke in.

"You leave me alone," I snapped, half-sobbing in my anger. "You started all this. You damned Butlers had to run to the king and make trouble."

"I didn't, Lady Margaret, I swear," he said patiently.

"Well, you're ready enough to obey the king's command," I snapped. "What kind of man are you, anyhow, to want a woman who abhors your entire family?"

His lips tightened a little at that, and I thought his eyes flashed pridefully. But he contented himself with a wintry smile.

I whirled around from him and faced Father again, abruptly changing my tactics.

"Father, you'd not give one of Juno's pups to him; how can you think of giving me?" I cried, trying to look small and helpless. I blinked rapidly, managing to blink up two tears, which I squeezed out and down my hot cheeks. "Why, it would be like pairing a poor little dove with a hawk . . ."

Mother burst out laughing. "Which would be the dove and which the hawk, pray? Ah, Magheen, why are you behaving in this wild, shameful way? Piers is a fine young man; a blind girl could see that. His blood is as old and honorable as yours. His ancestors were stewards to the first Plantagenets. They bear the oldest title in Ireland."

"I don't care if they were stewards to God," I burst out more characteristically. "Father, I have always obeyed you until now . . ."

"Always obeyed me? By Saint Bride, that's funny. And how dare you shame me so before our guests?"

"What do you care about the cursed Butlers? How can you do this to me? Ah, Father, you speak to me of shame. I'd think you couldn't lay your head down on your pillow tonight and sleep for shame at what you're trying to do. I think you're a coward. Afraid of the Butlers and the Tudor king . . ."

But I had gone too far.

"Magheen, shut up!" he roared.

I did so immediately, for there was steel in his voice, not fire. He stared at me furiously.

"Magheen, the saints alone know where you got that vile temper," he thundered.

"It's no great mystery to me, Gerald," Grandfather Fitz-Eustace said wryly, speaking for the first time. He and Mother were the only ones who could say such a thing without inviting Father's ire. With an effort, Father smiled now, a bit shamefacedly.

"Can't you see, lass, that we have no choice in the matter?" Mother said.

Sir James was smiling. But Piers arose from his place and curtly motioned his cousin to rise too.

"We'll leave you alone to make your family arrangements now," he said dryly, avoiding my eyes.

Reluctantly, Sir James arose and withdrew along with Piers and their retainers. Our own people and Eleanor, suddenly embarrassed at the fiery fight, shuffled to their feet and left the hall too. We three were left alone on the dais.

"Father," I said more moderately when we were left to ourselves, "you didn't mean it, did you? I don't have to marry him, do I?"

"Don't start on me, Magheen," he cried miserably. "Your mother's right; we've no choice in the matter. The king's been harassing me for years, ever since the Simnel affair. It's a mercy he's not taken Gerry hostage or imprisoned me in the Tower. I'm as courageous as the next man, but I've no choice. Surely you can understand that. If I refuse, he'll take it as further rebellion and clap me in the Tower and make you marry Piers anyhow. At least he's a decent lad. Thank the saints he didn't command you to marry Sir James."

"You'd have given me to *him*?" I screeched. "God, Father, that I should live to see this day."

"Then you think Piers might be a shade better than his cousin?" Father said with a wry grin, catching the nuance.

"That's like giving me a choice between the ocean and a whale to gobble me up, Father," I said bitterly. "Butlers are Butlers."

Mother sighed. "You're exactly alike," she said sadly. "Good lovers and good haters. And don't you know yet that they're all one and the same feeling? Just opposite ends of it. You must teach yourself to move from hate to love . . ."

"Mother, you talk nonsense. What do you know about it? Often you have told me Grandfather let you marry who you wanted. It's easy for you to preach at me . . ."

"Goddamn it, miss, don't be impertinent to your mother," Father said, but he glanced at her a bit shamed-facedly, as if thinking that they'd loved each other distractedly from their childhood, almost.

Seeing his thoughts in his eyes, as I always could, I softened my tone.

"Father, all my life I wanted to find a man I could love as Mother loves you," I said flatteringly. "From my cradle, I wanted a husband who'd make me happy as you have Mother."

At my words, he glanced down at her bright head beneath the simple white coif and wouldn't raise his eyes to meet mine. But I had seen the shamed pain in them.

"Magheen," Mother said chidingly, tears in her eyes, "please don't put your father through this. It's unfair, entirely. You're old enough to know that you must make *yourself* happy. If you go about expecting someone else to do it for you, you'll never find happiness. Especially is this true for women."

"That's easy for you to say, Mother; Father worships you," I retorted bitterly. "And you, yourself, told me you've loved him since you were a tiny girl."

"Father had betrothed me to him when I was only ten," she said quietly. "Until then, I'd had childish dreams of marrying his cousin, Maurice Fitzgerald."

Father laughed awkwardly. "Aye. I felt constrained to beat him at every tournament for years to prove my superiority," he confessed.

"But the point is that when I knew I was to marry your father, I began learning what there was about him to love," Mother continued. "I came to see that my father and mother were wiser than I; they had chosen for me the man I could be happy with for a lifetime."

"But you haven't chosen *my* husband; the King of England has," I persisted bitterly.

"Aye, Magheen," Mother said with uncharacteristic steel in her voice. "And so I want you to stop tormenting your father with these bitter accusations right now."

I bowed my head, and this time the tears that rolled down my cheeks were genuine. I knew that she was right. Father had been in trouble ever since the Tudor king had defeated Richard III at Bosworth. It had been a miracle that Grandfather FitzEustace, Uncle James Fitzgerald, and Father himself hadn't been tried for treason after the Simnel rebellion.

I went to Father and kissed him contritely. "I'm sorry, Father. I crave your pardon," I said miserably, wondering if I might be able to run away to a nunnery.

But nuns were not permitted to ride horseback or swim naked in some hidden forest pool or stuff themselves with sweetmeats on Twelfth Night. Nor would they ever lie content in a man's arms.

I knew that, although I'd not yet done the latter, I'd enjoy it entirely. Or would have, had I been allowed to choose for myself. Piers Butler's lean form and animated face rose in my mind and I flushed angrily. How could I submit to him?

"Don't grieve so, Magheen; it will be all right, you'll see," Father said, patting me ineffectually. "I wish to God there was a way I could keep my promise to let you choose for yourself. If it was only me, darling, I'd let the king be damned before I'd do his bidding. But you must understand that if I fell, all Ireland would fall to the likes of Black James. You'd not have that, now, would you?"

"No, Father, I know my duty . . . to Ireland," I sighed and, turning away, strode from the hall with my head up.

CHAPTER 2

I wanted nothing more than to get away from everyone.

Only that morning I'd been carefree, waking to the morning, alive with anticipation of what the day would bring. Always there had been mostly good in my life. I had loved being a Fitzgerald, one of the noisy, bickering brood of us, and confident that, in God's good time, I'd meet a man I could love as my mother loved my father. Then, in my never-truly-thought-out dream, I'd settle close by and proceed to rear a noisy family of my own.

But first there'd be long, golden days of riding the Fitzgerald demesne lands, gossiping with Eleanor, flirting with the knights and squires at Maynooth, drawing the thousand and one lovely views of Ireland and trying to count the shades of green in the spring.

What a false paradise my parents had built for me! How betrayed I now felt!

I knew, of course, that most girls were betrothed in childhood, some as early as in their cradles, and married by the time they were fifteen or sixteen—as soon, in fact, as they seemed fairly full-grown. There was never any question of who they'd marry, for it was usually all settled before they understood what marriage truly was. So, while we Fitzgerald girls well understood how desirable we were in the marriage game, being daughters of the greatest family in Ireland, we'd felt no particular impetus toward marriage. True, there'd been many a young noble ask for our hands, but Father had airily declined, enjoying the presence of his large family and in no hurry to part with us. There was no hurry, he'd told Mother. Were not we his daughters? The greatest heiresses in Ireland? And beautiful as the May as well. We could take our time, look around, marry when we found one who pleased us well and whose rank matched our own. And we'd gone blithely our ways, confident as princesses in our rank and place in life.

And now, at the command of the King of England, I was to be married to a Butler! Bitterly I berated my parents for letting us think we were the masters of our own fate. How much better for me to have been betrothed to one of my Desmond or O'Neill cousins in childhood, for not even Henry of England could then have interfered.

I felt exactly like a meadow rose, not yet unbudded, shorn off by the reaper's scythe and cast into a dark haymow. Lately, perhaps belatedly, I'd been having dreams of a shadowy, romantic man who walked and rode with me, held me in his arms. I would awake, pleasantly disturbed and dreamy, lazily trying to remember if I'd seen his face in my dreams. There was always an impression of blue, blue eyes and fair hair and gentle mien.

Certainly not like Piers Butler's flaming red hair and dark, snapping eyes and mocking expression.

Blindly, I groped my way into Mother's pleasance, pausing only long enough to snatch up my cloak, for the evening was damp and cold. I sank down on a stone bench along the garden wall and gave way to passionate, angry tears.

"Ah, Magheen, I thought I'd find you here. Always you go back to the earth with your troubles, don't you, lass?"

I looked up to meet Grandfather FitzEustace's gentle, blue gaze. "Don't cry, darling, it's not the end of the world," he said, sitting down and putting one frail arm around my shoulder.

"It's the end of *my* world, Grandfather," I sobbed, turning to put my head on his shoulder. "How could it be otherwise?"

"You're not married yet, Magheen," he said spiritedly. "There's many a thing could happen before you are. The

Welshman isn't so sure of his throne, you see, or he'd not be pushing through these marriages uniting his adherents and his old enemies."

"But I don't have much time," I said mournfully. "I'm full-grown these three years and Sir Piers is back in Ireland, no further away now than Kilkenny. What's to prevent a quick marriage?"

He sighed and patted my shoulder. "Aye, lass, what, indeed? I do wrong to encourage you in your denial of the facts. I should be helping you to accept your fate. I've always been a soft old fool where my grandchildren are concerned, and I feel an especial closeness to you who are forever doodling with a crayon or trying to fashion a ballad the way I have always done. Perhaps I've done wrong to have filled your head with courtly tales and fantasies, let you escape from reality into romantic nonsense."

"Is wanting to marry where your heart dictates romantic nonsense?" I demanded, drawing back to search his face.

"When it runs counter to duty, Magheen," he said gently.

"Never did I think to hear you speak so, Grandfather," I said mournfully, "'Twas you who gave me my first book, *Le Morte Arthur*. You believe in true love as much as I."

"But, Magheen, few of us realize that true love doesn't just happen but has to be cultivated," he said wisely. "I was a romantic old fool to let you ever think other. I thought it did you no harm to dream your young girl's dreams. But now I see I've hurt you."

I leaned down and pulled off a handful of drying lavender, tearing it to pieces, and, even in my agitation, breathing pleasurably deep of the sharp, clean scent. "Not you, Grandfather, not you. Father is the one who's hurt me," I said bitterly.

"That's not fair, Magheen. You know your father would never deliberately hurt you. And how could he dream the English king would demand you marry with Piers Butler? But since he has, you must not blame him for acquiescing."

"He'd force me to marry his enemy just to stay out of trouble," I insisted.

Grandfather sighed deeply and stared at me in some exasperation. I glanced furtively into his blue eyes, somewhat astonished that he'd find any fault with me, for in his eyes we children could do no wrong.

"You know he has no choice, Magheen," he said patiently. "Do you want to see him beheaded as a traitor?"

"Of course not, but . . ."

"Well, then, lass, grow up and realize his position. We all skirted pretty close to the wind in the Simnel affair, and the king hasn't truly trusted us since. Your father defied him after the lad was defeated and exposed as a pretender by leading us all in refusing to swear our fidelity to the Crown on our lands. It was beyond belief that he forced the king's representative, Dick Edgecombe, to accept our vows of fealty on the Sacrament and not on our lands. He saw that the king would use the slightest sign of disloyalty as an excuse for taking our lands and titles away and giving them to his Lancastrian English friends and stood his ground.

"But he's gone as far as he dares. His back is truly against the wall now and he knows it. You do wrong to accuse him of not caring about you agreeing to the marriage. After all, Piers Butler's blood is the best in Ireland, and he's a fine lad as well."

"Grandfather, you sound just like Mother and Father," I cried angrily. "You think a mighty lot of my father; well, if he's such a great and influential man, why doesn't he put himself at the head of the wild Irish and fight the English king and his people? They'd crown *him* King of Ireland in a wink."

I had expected a shocked exclamation at the least, but Grandfather only looked at me bemused. "You think the marital fate of a slip of a girl would cause him to betray his trust? Nay, darling, even when he was in outright rebellion against the king it wasn't for his own advancement; he believed the boy we had here was truly the English

Earl of Warwick. You know your father better than that."
He took my chin in his hand and turned my face toward
his. "Magheen, Magheen, you're no Helen of Troy to have
nations warring because of you; I'm ashamed you'd think
such a thing."

Subdued, I would not meet his eyes. It did indeed
shame me to have Grandfather disappointed in me. "Nay,
Grandfather," I said at last grudgingly, "I would not be
the cause of war. But it isn't fair, all the same."

"It's the way of the world, child. What would become of
our society if alliances couldn't be made by marriage? The
nobility have privileges above the lesser classes, but, you
see, they have greater responsibilities too. And if any of us
shirks his duty, there'd be chaos."

"But we've hearts like the peasants, Grandfather," I
cried. "Why is it asking too much to marry someone you
love?"

"No, if you're not a stubborn maid, you can come to love
him who's chosen for you."

"Just like that," I said bitterly. "Well, I *am* a stubborn
maid and I can't learn to love whom I despise. The Tudor
king and . . . and our society may force me to marry Piers
Butler, but I'll never give him my love. I'll . . . I'll shrivel
up and die, pickled in my own bile, and he'll never touch
me; by the rood, I swear it."

He took my hand, which was damp and cold at once,
between his warm and dry ones. "You'll change your
mind, Magheen, you'll see. He's a fine lad and always was.
Like your father, I remember him when he was a little
knave. Nor could I help but be impressed with him in t'hall
just now. He means to treat you well and honorably and
doesn't hold it against you that you're a Fitzgerald . . ."

"And why on earth should he?" I flared. "Why should
he not be proud to have a Fitzgerald in *his* scurvy family?"

"At least your father has instilled family pride into you,"
he said with a chuckle. "But you must realize his blood
and lineage are as good as your own."

"If I hear one more time that his lineage is as good as

Gerait's Daughter 5-28-97   29

mine, I'll scream," I snapped. "I thought you at least
would be on my side, Grandfather. Old as you were at the
time, you still fought for the Yorkists at Stoke field."

"And would again, sweetheart, were there one of them
to ride for. I mislike the idea of a Lancastrian on the
throne too. But we have no other," he said sadly.

I sat staring down at our intertwined hands. He was
right, of course. There was no use defying King Henry; he
was our lawful, annointed king. There was no qualified
Yorkist.

But it wasn't in my nature to make the best of it. I crept
away to bed vowing I'd make Piers Butler wish he'd never
heard of Margaret Fitzgerald.

The two Butlers sailed away to Waterford the next day,
promising to return in a day or two for the betrothal ceremony. I thought of running away but, despite my wild
threats to go Irish, I knew there really was no place to run.

Nor, in truth, could I find it in my heart to betray my father's trust that I'd do my duty to him and our family.

The Butlers were back at Saint Thomas Court by Allhal-
lows'een. When I saw Piers's blue-and-gold standard flut-
tering through the gate at the end of his attendant's lance,
I ran away to the library, which was my customary retreat
when trying to escape little Gerry's entreaties for bedtime
stories.

But Mother, knowing so well where I'd be, traitorously
sent Sir Piers to find me there.

He knocked peremptorily at the door, then, without
waiting for permission, pushed it open and walked in.
Something green and lustrous and rich hung across his
right arm.

"I beg your pardon for intruding, Lady Margaret, but I
have brought you a wedding gift."

"I want no gift from you," I said stiffly, pretending
to read Father's copy of Virgil, which lay open on a table
under the window. "No one consulted me before arranging that I should marry you, no one listened to my objec-

tions when I was ordered to, and it's a mockery entirely for you to tender me a gift."

His face remained solemn, but I felt a sort of laughter in the keen brown eyes. Nevertheless, his voice was low and serious as he crossed the room and extended the rich, green stuff, now laid across both outstretched arms like a priest's vestments.

"All of which in no way diminishes my determination to present you with this rich cloth which I purchased in Waterford. I think it's remarkably suitable for your coloring."

In spite of wanting to appear indifferent entirely to the lustrous fabric, I felt my eyes drawn irresistibly. It was as sheen as the river Liffey on a clear day, the green of it deep and radiant as Irish grass in spring, say, just at the gloaming when the birdsong falls and the shadows lengthen to the height of ancient giants. Never had I seen cloth so lovely, so begging to be stroked. My fingers literally itched to reach out and touch it.

But the hated Butler was the bearer of it.

"If you think to gain my affections with a bit of rag . . ."

"Margaret, I'd not want your affections could they be so easily won," he interrupted. "Can't you just accept it in the interests of peace? If, by some unforeseen chance, the king should rescind his command that we wed, then, well, you can still make a wedding gown of it, whoever you marry."

"You're a poor-spirited wight to say a thing like that," I said scornfully. "How can I be content with a man who'd be such a ninny? Why, if my father gave a girl a length of cloth for a wedding gown and she married another in it, he'd smother her in the cursed thing!"

An angry red flush spread across his face and his jaw worked spasmodically. So he wasn't quite the dispassionate diplomat he'd have me believe. He had a measure of pride, after all.

He laid the fabric on the table beside the book and bowed stiffly.

"Suit yourself," he said coldly. "At least I have made a real effort for the sake of England and Ireland."

Stung by the coldness in his voice, although I'd certainly asked for it, I whirled away from him. "Take the stuff and make caparisons for your horses," I hissed.

But he was stalking from the room, shutting the door behind him, resolutely refusing to hear me.

I snatched up the fabric, determined to throw it on the fire, but its luster, its softness were too much for me. I paused, running my thumb along the length of it, entranced in spite of myself at the way the color changed in depth as the cloth moved, shimmering like the sea on a high, clear day.

"By the rood, 'twould be sacrilege, almost, to destroy it," I whispered huskily and put it down again. *I* could never bring myself to wear it, but Mother would be lovely in such a gown once her baby had been delivered and her waistline restored. And in a little while, when I was certain Sir Piers and the rest of the Butler retinue were being fed in the great hall, I slipped away to my room with the lovely stuff and folded it into my coffer.

I filled my pockets with apples from the storeroom and went out unseen, or so I hoped, not wanting to encounter any of the Butlers, to the stables beyond the courtyard.

Making sure the lads were all at supper, I saddled my horse myself and led her quietly across the field below the house and into the adjoining woods before I mounted, well knowing I was disobeying my father's orders that we girls never ride out alone.

The trees were nearly all bare, yet there was a warm, living atmosphere in the woods from the light reflecting off the carpet of golden and brown leaves. I rode slowly, savoring the time alone, away from the tensions in the castle. Not only the Butlers were there, but I'd seen servants in the livery of Walter Fitzsimmonds, the Archbishop of Dublin, in the retinue swarming over Saint Thomas Court. No doubt the Butlers had brought him along to finalize plans for the wedding. I thought sourly of the portly arch-

bishop. Father disliked him heartily, as he did most bishops, saying that the surest way to corrupt any of the
clergy was to award them a bishop's miter. Then they'd
quickly become as grasping and crafty as any prince in
Christendom. He'd good reason to believe so of Walter
Fitzsimmonds, for he was almost as quick to trot across
Saint George's Channel with tattling tales of Father's mis-
demeanors as Sir James himself.

And only too soon I'd be required to stand with Sir Piers
Butler before him and pledge vows of marriage.

I turned my horse toward the north and gazed off into
the gray misty distance, toward the wild O'Hanlon's lands.
If I were a man, I could ride off and join them. Or hunt for
my food, build a hut in some wild glen and live forever
alone.

But I knew that never would I be happy were I to shirk
my duty, betray my trust, leave my family and the other
Anglo-Irish to the king's wrath. I would obey the king and
marry the Butler. He'd never touch me, though, I thought
grimly. I would make his life so miserable that he'd be
glad to beg the king for permission to get an annulment.
Even the Church would agree to that when we both swore
the marriage had not been consummated. And perhaps
then the king would turn his attention to other matters.
What right had he to be arranging people's lives for them
anyhow?

I knew that if my absence from Saint Thomas Court was
noted, I'd be in trouble. Lionel Howth, one of Father's
guards at Saint Thomas Court or Maynooth when we were
at home, was our unofficial guardian. He was a gentle,
somewhat simple giant who could be like a bear gone
amok when he felt Father or any belonging to him were
threatened. He was even bigger than Father, with tightly
curled yellow hair that clung to his head like a sheep's
hide. His eyes were smallish and of an ambiguous green-
brown. His nose was flattened at the tip as if he'd run
somewhat precipitously into a barn wall. He was the illegitimate son of one of the Lord of Howth's younger

brothers, gotten on a servant girl who'd died shortly after
he was born. His father's legitimate wife wouldn't have
him in her household, and so Mother had taken him to rear
with us and, when he was old enough, Father had taken
him as squire and coached him until he won his spurs.
Later, his father had died, leaving him a bit of land
scarcely worthy of being called a demesne. But he'd
stayed on with us. He'd have died for Father and Mother.
And, fortunately for our freedom to ride where we would,
his devotion had extended to their children.

I was suddenly aware of the silence of the dim woods
and thought fleetingly that I should have routed Lionel
from the table to attend me. Yet dearly did he love his
meals, and, besides, I'd probably have encountered the
Butlers had I stopped in the hall to fetch him. Uneasily, I
realized the wild Irish had been known to invade even the
Pale. Within the wood, the feeble winter sun had surrendered entirely to the gloom. All around was silence and
the dying, drying forest. Occasionally a wood dove's
mournful call pierced the stillness, and sudden skitterings
spoke of squirrels busy against the coming winter.

Suddenly, from a knoll to my left, came a horse's quick,
surprised snort and, turning toward the sound, I met Sir
James Butler's baleful gaze.

"I thought I saw you cross the quadrangle toward the
stables," he said with satisfaction. "It was worth a short
ride to chance catching you to myself."

"Well, now you have, you can ride straight back, for I've
nothing to say to you and your ilk," I said grimly.

"The king has commanded us to peace, Lady Margaret,
and since we'll soon be cousins, you must greet me right
cousinly."

"There'll be peace in Ireland if you leave us alone," I
snapped. "My father says you no more than set foot on
Irish soil than the O'Neill or the O'Donnell are in harness
and riding against each other or someone in the Pale."

"Your father shouldn't blame me if he can't do his job,"
he said complacently. "It's his place to beat the wild Irish

into line, and if he can't, there are better men willing and able to do so."

"Yourself, you no doubt mean," I scoffed. "All you do is start yet another battle. Father rules with an iron hand yet conciliates, gets the wild Irish to reason together."

"He's only a damned Irishman himself."

"And you're only a damned Butler. On the best day of your miserable life you couldn't fill my father's shoes."

He'd edged his horse down the knoll to stand beside me. Warily, I drew my own mount back.

"Don't be aloof, Margaret, I'll soon be your cousin. Though, by the rood, I'd sooner be your husband," he said smoothly.

"Ha. That day the sun would rise in the west," I scoffed, wheeling away from him. "Had the king ordered me to marry *you*, I'd have incited the O'Hanlon to violence against you. They'd have followed me too. I'm Gerait More's daughter, after all."

Laughing, he lunged forward and seized my horse's bridle, so deftly I scarcely knew how he'd captured it. I tried to wheel away, lifting my riding crop against him, but he dodged skillfully, drawing my horse ever closer to his side.

"God, you're luscious. A kiss, sweet cousin."

"You're risking death, you fool," I cried, jerking at my reins.

"From whom? Your father or my bookish cousin?"

"From me had I taken time to arm myself before riding out," I said.

I was growing uneasy despite my bold words. What a fool I'd been to venture out alone. Surely he'd not dare to lay a hand on me. He was only enjoying my discomfort, wasn't he? Yet the more I struggled to free myself, the harder he held me. If I were to escape him, I thought, it would have to be by cunning.

I relaxed, ceased to pull on the reins. Seeing this, Sir James relaxed too, but leaned closer still as if to kiss me. I pretended to await his caress and, when he was inches from my face, shouted at the top of my lungs.

"Croom-abo!" I yelled.

Startled, he dropped my reins and I lost no time in wheeling my horse and galloping up the knoll away from him.

I heard him swear furiously, then wheel in pursuit. I turned back toward Saint Thomas Court, riding furiously. His big stallion, fleeter and more powerful than my small Irish cob, would have quickly overtaken me but I continued to sound the Fitzgerald battle cry, pounding for the nethergate.

A horseman was coming hard toward me. Straining my eyes in the gloaming, I saw that it was Sir Piers. A welcome rescuer indeed, I thought stormily. But at least he'd not let the detestable Sir James have me.

"Lady Margaret, what mean you, riding out like this alone?" he snapped. "Your father is hunting the castle for you . . ." He stopped short, seeing his cousin in pursuit.

"Aye, your black cousin has accosted me," I flared, slowing to a halt. "I'd resent your tone, but you're too well come. I know not what would have befallen me had you not."

Sir Piers's hand flew to the small dagger at his waist.

"What have you been about, James?" he said furiously.

"The lady misunderstood my intentions," Sir James said smoothly. "I meant only to escort her safely back to Saint Thomas Court. How could you think I'd wish ill to my cousin's betrothed?"

Piers stared at us uncertainly.

"You know how truthful *he* is," I snapped. "But no matter; I've learned my lesson and won't venture out again without an armed guard so long as your black cousin is in Ireland. Why is my father hunting for me?"

"There's a message from the quay," Sir Piers said. "Your father's cousin, Maurice of Desmond, has come from Cork with a visitor. He . . ."—here he stopped and shook his head in bafflement—". . . he actually bids your father come forward with the best escort he can muster to greet

His Grace, Richard Plantagenet, Duke of York and heir to the Kingdom of England and Ireland."

For a long moment, neither Sir James nor I made a sound. In truth, I could not have spoken had my life depended upon it. Richard of York! He was the younger of King Edward's sons. Men said they'd been murdered by his uncle, Richard of Gloucester, who'd then taken the throne as Richard III. No one had ever heard of either boy since they'd entered the Tower in 1483, more than seven years ago.

Yet there'd been rumors that one of them had escaped. Could it be possible? Could this stranger be Richard Plantagenet, Duke of York? Or was it just another chimera? Another pretend boy advanced by Margaret of Burgundy because she hated Henry of England with a violent passion?

I fervently prayed it was the former.

But the Butlers had heard of his existence. They knew that he was here in Ireland and would waste no time telling King Henry. Why had not Cousin Maurice chosen his time with more care? He was nicknamed "the bellicose," and it was apt indeed. His impetuosity was likely to bring Henry's wrath down on us before we could ascertain the justice of the newcomer's cause.

Nervously, I looked from one to the other of the Butlers.

"I suppose you'll waste no time crossing the channel with this information," I said doggedly. "Just make sure you tell your Tudor king that my father had nothing to do with this; I know it's all a surprise to him."

Sir James's eyes were gloating. "Of course. Your father is a blessed innocent and wouldn't dream of scheming against the king," he said sarcastically. "Lucky we were here when Maurice's messenger arrived."

"You won't cause us any trouble," I cried anxiously. "My father's agreed to marry me to Sir Piers. What more can we do to show subjection?"

"You've certainly changed your tone, maiden," Sir James said maliciously, "now that you realize we've got you."

"For the love of God, leave the girl alone," Sir Piers said unexpectedly. "We've no proof her father sent for this new boy. Nor any reason to badger her about it if he did."

"You're a fool, Piers, if you don't realize the Fitzgeralds would do anything to have a Yorkist, real or pretend, back on the throne. You know how little His Majesty trusts them; take care you don't lose his trust, too, by showing undue tolerance to them."

"I'm only saying there's no point in seeing a treason plot hatching under every bush in Ireland," was the laconic reply.

"I'm off to England, at any rate; and if you know what's good for you, you'll come too. Leave these traitors to their fate."

"Don't be a fool, James," Piers drawled. "I'm staying here in Ireland to take control of my uncle's affairs, as the king bade me. There's no reason for all this uproar. Kildare's not likely to be taken in again by one of Madam Margaret's parade of masquers, and the king won't thank you for making mountains out of molehills. You know his policy is to laugh these lads to scorn."

But Sir James's eyes narrowed balefully. "Suit yourself. I sail with the tide. Don't say you weren't warned."

With that, he whirled away, threw his reins to a waiting attendant, and dismounted, all in one smooth motion. He strode into the castle, calling to his people to pack his belongings immediately.

Piers and I were left standing together on the stairs.

"I have the feeling the day will come I'll rue not slitting his self-serving neck right here," he said almost to himself.

I glanced up at him uncertainly. He was a member of the family which had been enemy to mine for generations, yet he'd come to my father's defense.

"I thank you for your defense," I said grudgingly. "I . . . I haven't given you much cause to so do, but I thank you all the same." Then, not wanting him to think I had changed my mind about him, I sniffed a little and added,

"Just like a Butler, though, to try to make something out of nothing for his own advantage."

The brown eyes had seemed to soften for a barely perceptible moment, but at the last remark they filled with mocking laughter.

"Oh, I've no doubt my cousin was right in his evaluation of your family," he said, "but I see no point in stirring up the king with no proof or cause. Chances are, your father will be smart enough to know this lad has no more chance than the last of taking the throne from Henry and, so, won't be likely to throw in his lot again."

"Oh, you're . . . you're just despicable," I cried. "I'm glad *I* don't take such a cynical view of everyone's motives. If my father thought this lad had a right to the throne of England, he'd back him if the boy had nothing but the shoes he stood in!" I snapped my teeth shut hard as I realized how my anger had made me blurt out a statement that could only harm Father in the king's eyes.

The cursed Butler, quick to read each word and thought, broke into a hearty laugh. "Your own words corroborate what I've just said, Lady Margaret. 'Twere a fool, indeed, to put one's health and well-being in a Fitzgerald's hands."

And before I could answer him, he turned on his heel and ran up the stairs to the entrance, leaving me seething alone.

I found Father and Grandfather FitzEustace in the library, discussing the unexpected message from the harbor.

"Could what Madam Margaret says be true, Gerald?" Grandfather was saying. "After Stoke, I thought perhaps the Simnel boy had been but a stalking horse for her nephew, the Earl of Lincoln. Yet she sent him along with the army and he died at Stoke. Could she have had Richard of York there in Burgundy all along? Could the Simnel boy have been stalking horse to the real heir to England?"

Father strode back and forth, shaking his shaggy head

in bafflement. "I wish I knew, Milord Father, I wish I knew," he said.

"We're going to see him, aren't we, Father?" I asked. "We will never know if he's truly Prince Richard until we see him and talk to him."

"I don't know," he said worriedly. "I'm weary of trouble; I don't relish courting it over another pretender."

"But you must. How will you know if he's a pretender else?" I said, taking his arm. "Please, Father, I've accepted that I have to marry a Butler . . . or *had* accepted it. But if there's a true prince of England still about, then, oh, don't you see? I won't *have* to do as the Lancastrian king says."

Grandfather's blue eyes crackled with excitement.

"By heaven, Gerald, she's right; you owe it to Magheen to at least investigate this lad's claims."

Father stopped pacing and stared down at me. "It would please me much to send Sir James packing," he conceded. "Although I still think Piers is a decent enough sort."

"But a Butler, Father," I prodded. "You'd not be joining our house with the Butlers if you could help it, now, would you?"

He grinned and hugged me.

"You're a witchy-welf. I couldn't think of a greater revenge on the Butlers than to bestow you upon them, but, yes, Magheen, we'll greet the lad who says he's Richard of York. Take him to Maynooth for Eleanor's betrothal. Irish hospitality demands no one be turned away lest Christ turn us from heaven. And so I'll tell King Henry if he chides me."

I kissed and hugged both Father and Grandfather happily. But conscience made me tell them Sir James was on his way to England with word of the visitor.

Father frowned and chewed his lip.

"No more than I expected," he said slowly. "I doubt he can harm us. After all, he has my sworn promise to marry you to Piers to hand to the king. And he well knows I didn't send for this boy."

But as I went to freshen up before riding to the harbor, I wondered if King Henry would believe that after Sir James was through reporting.

Curse all Butlers, I thought distractedly. I hoped the man we were riding to greet would be so princely, have such warmth and commanding charm that all Ireland and England would rise against the Tudor king in his behalf.

Piers and his retinue were mounted, ready to leave, when we went out to the courtyard to ride to the harbor.

"Gerait More, I see that you're foolish enough to greet this newcomer," Piers said stonily.

"As Deputy of Ireland, it's his duty to greet all newcomers who claim royal rank," I said defensively. "You can't fault him for that."

"Margaret, will you let me answer for myself?" Father snapped. Then, laughing ruefully, he turned to Piers, drawing on his charm to avoid a direct answer. "God's bones, man, I can almost find it in my heart to pity you that you've agreed to marry this spitfire. If you knew what was in store for you, chances are you'd be riding under the lad's banner yourself to avoid such a fate."

"There's nothing funny about this situation, milord," Piers snapped, suddenly angry. "You're getting yourself into a mess, and perhaps other innocent people as well. I am warning you to stay free of any such entanglement."

"Who are you to warn my father?" I said, though Father's laughing words had stung. "You're just afraid of losing your favored place with the king and of the chance to marry into our family."

This brought a scornful laugh.

"There seems to be no limit to your good opinion of yourselves," he said, eyes snapping with malicious laughter. "Well, I've said my say and no man can do more. Your actions be on your own head, Kildare."

And, in his maddening way, he whirled and galloped

through the gate, his men at his horse's heels, having, as usual, had the last word.

The retinue Father took was goodly enough for a king of England, I thought with satisfaction. Besides Father and Grandfather, there was my Uncle James Fitzgerald, Father's younger brother, who was much as Father had been five years before; my Uncle Thomas FitzEustace, Mother's brother, a big, silent man with a pointed mustache and sharp, blue eyes that misted often with sentiment despite his own conviction that he was tough and inscrutable; Lionel, Walter Delahide, Jimmy Boyce, and our chaplain, Brother Joseph. I rode among them with pride. How fine and strong and handsome were the men of Ireland. I prayed this Yorkist Prince would be worthy to lead them against Henry of England.

I gazed about me at the rain-blown November landscape, glowing in the late-afternoon sun. For all it was shadowed somewhat by massing silver-gray clouds and the trees stood stark against the fading light, it was the most beautiful land on earth. The hills rolled off into soft gray sky like the gentle curves of Mother's face, and each dark rock, each stunted growth of tree, each quick flash of golden light through breaks in the clouds, each bent peasant cutting peat in low-lying bogs, spoke to me of my deep and abiding love for Ireland. They said we Anglo-Irish had become more Irish than the Irish. Aye. It was so. Why did we have to be tossed and blown by English whim and English politics? I wished passionately that Father would declare himself King of Ireland and accept the enthusiastic backing of all the Irish. Then I could marry whom I chose.

But I knew it was a silly girl's dream. As Grandfather FitzEustace had pointed out, Father saw himself as an English subject albeit Irish in personal preference.

Grandfather and Walter chatted easily about the coming Parliament and the matters that would be taken under consideration. Salt had recently risen to the unheard-of price of a groat a pound, and something had to be done about the untoward cost of goods. Revenues would have to be voted to buy new weapons for the Guild of Saint George, because the depredations of the wild Irish were getting bolder. And now, of course, there would be discussion of the new visitor to Ireland.

"How I hope he truly *is* Richard of York," Grandfather was saying. "And with one tenth his father's dash and good sense. Ah, Walter, you should have seen the goodly look of King Ned in his youth. So bold and comely. There was never the wisp of a doubt that he was a king, I can tell you. Next to him, this frail Tudor is a pusillanimous clerk."

I smiled at his words. If ever there was a frail man, it was the little bird that was Grandfather. He perched like one atop the gentle old cob he always rode. Yet there was never the slightest doubt that *he* was the proud Lord of Portlester, either. His few remaining cronies had long since retired to their firesides, but Grandfather still rode the Pale at Father's side, eliciting the admiration and respect of all. Still, he was in his eighties and the November wind was cold.

"Are you warm enough, Grandfather?" I said impulsively, though I knew he didn't like being fussed over.

His eyes laughed at me. "Of course, Magheen. Don't be thinking I need a posset and a blanket yet."

Father grinned. "*I'll* need them before *you*, Milord Father," he said.

We had reached the harbor, and a Flemish trade ship lay there at anchor. Father's cousin Maurice, a tall, rangy, dark-haired firebrand of a man in Irish garb, stood leaning against a post, as if watching for us.

"Cousin, wait till you see him," Maurice cried, striding toward us excitedly. "It's like Edward reborn, I swear."

"Well, where is he?" Father said. "We thought he was waiting for us."

"He's having a last conference aboard ship with his advisers, Sir John Taylor and Sir Edward Skelton. He'll be along directly."

Father's face formed an expression of being impressed. "Sir John Taylor was one of King Edward's most trusted men. If he thinks this lad is Richard, he ought to know. Skelton I never heard of."

Walter was eyeing a waterfront inn expectantly.

"Your father-in-law's cold and tired, Gerait More. Why do not we wait for the duke within by the fire?" he said.

Father laughed. "Father-in-law is't? You'd not be wanting a drop to warm yourself, would you, Wat? Well, the idea's sound, whoever concurs. Maurice, tell one of your people to bring the duke and his party to us within the King's Pale yonder."

The inn stood on a little knoll, with a window that overlooked the harbor and the Flemish ship lying by. We dismounted and went in where a peat fire made smoky heat. I went and stood by the fire, not wanting to drink of the ale or "water of life" or whiskey the innkeeper soon brought for the men.

Walter, always garrulous, soon launched into telling of seeing all the souls of those drowned in the sea floating below the outer ward of Maynooth the previous Whitsuntide.

"They were riding across the heath on ghastly white horses, trailin' their shrouds, men souls, women souls, and little baby souls," he said wonderingly, downing another measure. "Trailin' their shrouds, they were."

Grandfather, who dearly loved a ghost story and got a little tight on a mere measure of ale, hiccuped and rubbed a finger along his thin nose.

"The horses or the souls were trailing the shrouds, Wat?" he asked.

"The souls, of course. Of all them that were drowned in the seas."

"If they were drowned in the seas, who put 'em in their shrouds?" Grandfather asked shrewdly and winked at me as if to say, "See, Magheen, *I'm* not drunk."

The door of the inn opened suddenly, admitting a blast of frigid, sea-laden air. Maurice and several of his people crowded into the room, excitement in their bearing. They stood aside as if to make an aisle of honor and swept their bonnets from their heads.

"Milord of Kildare, Gerait More, 'tis my great honor to present you to His Grace, Richard Plantagenet, Duke of York, heir to the Kingdoms of England and France and the Lordship of Ireland," he cried dramatically, turning to the doorway where stood framed a tall, blond young man in a magnificent blue costume. His face was shielded from my sight by a great ostrich plume that swept down from the top of the cap, but his form and bearing were splendid, his smooth, fair hair the consistency of silken skeins.

Father was standing directly in front of the young man and he drew a deep, shocked breath, audible to me at my post by the fire.

"God's splendor, Milord Father, he's the image of Edward," he whispered in a voice that might have been a shout.

Grandfather moved forward shakily, peering up into the newcomer's face.

"Aye, Gerald," he said wonderingly. "For certain, the apple didn't roll far from the tree. If he's not Richard of York, then one of Edward's many bastards, I'd swear."

My heart was beating painfully. They believed he was the Plantagenet prince. The true heir to England. This lordly man, not Henry Tudor, should be sitting on England's throne. I felt as if heaven had heard my frantic pleas of the last few days. The fact that to put this lad where he belonged would require a major war seemed incidental to me at that moment. At least he seemed to be whom he said he was. All other explanations I quickly dismissed. Father and the other barons would be willing to follow him, and I would be freed of the necessity of marrying Piers Butler. I put my hand to my mouth to prevent crying out a joyful Te Deum.

The young man drew his cap from his head in a singularly graceful gesture, smiling to show firm white teeth. His eyes, beneath spun-gold lashes and brows, were the same startling royal blue of his velvet clothes, and as they swept the room, finally meeting my own, I realized with heart-stopping certainty that they were also the eyes of the handsome, gentle lover I'd begun to dream of.

CHAPTER 3

Mother, well-advanced in her pregnancy, took Lionel, the three younger children, and a small band on to Maynooth the following morning, leaving Eleanor and me to see to the closing of Saint Thomas Court. We would follow when Parliament was over, with Father's retinue and the Duke's for, though she'd already retired to her bower when we came back to the Court and had departed for Maynooth before he arose the following morning, she'd left word that he was to spend Christmas with us at our favorite castle. At least, I thought with satisfaction, Mother and Father were inclined to listen to the young man. How I prayed he'd convince them of his identity truly being the Duke of York!

I never doubted it from the first.

He spoke wittily and articulately of his life as a child at Westminster with King Edward and Queen Elizabeth and his many sisters. He recounted details of that long-ago life that only a true Plantagenet prince could have known. Eagerly I watched Father and Grandfather, who'd been good friends of Edward IV, for signs of acceptance, but though they freely acknowledged the "lad" was the very image of Edward IV when first he'd come to the throne, they were both noncommittal entirely about anything further than that.

Yet, he was invited to Maynooth for Christmas.

Throughout the week of Parliament, I found myself falling more and more deeply under the young man's spell. I had heard it said that Edward IV was so charming and comely he could have had, for the asking, any woman in

England. The number of illegitimate children he had corroborated the truth of this. As I came to know the young Duke of York, I thought that if Edward had had one tenth his charm, it was no wonder women adored him. Yet never once did Richard behave toward me in the lascivious way that had made his father notorious.

Still, I felt that he was coming to reciprocate my well-concealed feelings toward him. I began to dream wild dreams of marrying Richard and riding into battle beside him as Red Eva had done with her husband, Strongbow. Together, we'd recapture his kingdom.

But in my saner moments I knew we'd have to have much aid, arms, money and men. I knew it was imperative for Father and the other barons to believe him and back him.

When Parliament adjourned on December 5, Saint Nicholas Eve, we started for Maynooth, though it was twelve miles distant and past nones before we were able to leave. Father was adamant about waiting for morning.

"By Saint Bride," he said to the duke, "when work is done and I'm free to return to the Lady Allison, I'm like a tired and hungry horse given his head to return to stall and oats. She'll be waiting and her time is nearly nigh."

So it was well past the hour of the evening meal before we reached Maynooth. A light snow had started to fall, and the castle materialized out of the dark like some fairy dwelling shimmering amid the swirling snow. Father hailed the gateward, who shouted in acknowledgment and lifted the portcullis in the outer wall. We clattered across the bridge and into the courtyard.

Nell and I slid down, leaving our horses to the stable boys who ran to help us. The men alighted and tossed their reins toward the boys, but, in truth, the animals needed no more urging than Father to go to their favorite place and trotted off, heads down and snorting in anticipation.

I stared up at the Fitzgerald arms above the door. The

apes, salient aflank the shield, seemed to have white fur mantles and caps from the snow.

Father opened the double doors and we crowded into the small chamber within, glad to escape the rising wind. The portcullis was up, just inside these doors. On the left, a heavy door covered the stairway down to the guardroom and cellars, and on the right another door barred the stairway to the second story. Straight ahead was the door to the great hall. All were kept barred from the other side for easier defense of the castle. As Father closed the doors behind us, a missile whipped past my cheek and the screeching, dropping portcullis would have cut Father in two had he not leaped back, nearly knocking Jimmy Boyce down.

"In the name of heaven, what's happening?" cried Richard's priest-companion, Sir John Taylor, throwing himself in front of the duke.

"It's Alice, Father," I said, for by now I realized the stone that had almost hit me had been hurled from the murdering hole built above the entrance to all Irish castles for the purpose of surprising would-be attackers and had looked up to see my little sister's hoydenish face quickly withdrawing.

"Alice, by Saint Bride, I'll tan you good," Father yelled furiously. "Get you down out of that hole and let us in."

We heard her scurrying like a frightened squirrel, and the trapdoor dropped into place with a thud. Then the noises moved away within the castle and down the ladder inside the front door. In a moment the inner doors opened and Alice's square little form stood silhouetted against the light from torch and fire and candle.

Father picked her up roughly and administered a quick, light slap to her backside, then kissed her warmly before setting her down.

"No wonder our sire can't cure us of wrongdoing," Eleanor whispered, chuckling softly. "That beating really hurt her, didn't it?"

"Now witchy-welf, what do you mean, pelting us like

that? You nearly tore my hands off!" Father demanded, ushering the rest of us into the hall.

"I'm sorry, Father, but you should ha' sent word that you'd be home this night," Alice said spiritedly. "And me alone, here, to defend my lady-mother against the murdering Butlers and such. I'd heard the horses in the court and strange voices . . ."—here she glanced accusingly at Richard and his people—". . . and climbed up into the murdering hole to give them a proper welcome."

Father's eyes were twinkling wildly, but he kept his expression suitably stern.

"I've told you a hundred times, lass, *all* are to be treated with hospitality. Don't you remember the poem I read you?

"Oh King of stars!
Whether my house be dark or bright,
Never shall it be closed against anyone,
Lest Christ should close His house against me."

"And does that even mean the damned, thieving, murdering Butlers, Father?" she said shrewdly, squinting up at him with big witching eyes.

In spite of himself, Father exploded into a loud guffaw and pulled Alice into a tight hug.

"So you'd be braining a Butler, then, lass. Well, best you call the guard in future. And what do you mean by saying you're alone to guard your mother? There are a hundred armed men at Maynooth if there's one. You *know* the gateward would never have admitted Butlers."

"He could have been overpowered, milord," Alice said stubbornly.

"Who lowered the portcullis? *You* surely couldn't manage that alone," Eleanor said.

"Michael," Alice admitted, at which one of the bigger pages came around the corner of the entrance recess, eyes downcast.

"Are you pisky-witched, lad? Must you always do this mad maid's bidding?" Father cried, but Michael, expert from long practice in diverting Father's wrath, scuffed his feet and cleared his throat.

"The Lady Allison's gone off to see to the little lad's bedtime, milord. Shall I call her?"

Father rose to the bait.

"Aye, call her right away. Then tell the kitchens we're hungry." He strode down the middle of the hall, shouting for food and more fire and attendance, and in moments the room was swarming with castle people, taking our cloaks and baggage, pushing the newly brought-in Yule log more deeply within the fireplace and piling peat upon it to help it blaze, laying trenchers, and, in the case of three musicians, scrambling into the minstrels gallery with lute and atabout and rebec, which were soon playing melodiously.

At Michael's summons, Mother came from above, down the far stairs, looking ponderous and weary. Father bounded toward her as she dropped him a clumsy curtsy, huge gray eyes shadowed and sparkling with joy as she gazed up at him. He pulled her up and, great mound and all, into his muscular arms for a long embrace.

"Milord, our guests!" Mother cried in a muffled voice from the depths of his hug. "Release me, pray. But I'm glad you're safely home."

"'Tis only your endless prayers, beloved of heaven, that accomplish it, Lady, I'm sure," Father said, releasing her. He drew her forward, presenting her to the newcomers.

"Sir Richard Plantagenet, Sir John Taylor, my lady-wife, Lady Allison," Father said, studiously avoiding giving Richard the ducal title.

"Welcome to Maynooth, milords," Mother said, following suit and curtsying, this time holding Father's arm for support.

"I am your servant, Lady," Richard said, bowing. "I have heard much of your great beauty and charm. I am happy to see the reports were not exaggerated."

Mother smiled her acknowledgment of the compliment.

"I have ordered baths readied. But if you've had no dinner, perhaps you'd prefer to eat first. The fare is being prepared, though not as goodly as I'd have desired."

"Be damned to the baths until we've eaten," Father said, putting an arm around her shoulders and hugging her. "We're hungry enough to eat oatcakes and ale if you have no other."

Mother released herself, giving Father a quick, wafted kiss, and went to call the servants to wait on us. Only then did Nell and I manage a quick hug and a few words with her. Though Maynooth was overflowing with retainers and servants, pages and squires, still she was never idle but constantly directing, planning, brewing the medicines and simples needful for our health, and supervising the baking, cooking and laundry. Even when she sat down at day's end, there was usually a length of cloth and a needle in her hand.

She had managed to provide us with a toothsome repast, even on such short notice. There was a joint of beef and one of mutton, obviously held over a low fire in case we came home late, a pair of cold, boiled mallards, a custard with raisins and almonds, and lots of fresh-baked white bread and butter. Wine, mulled and spiced, eased and warmed us.

She didn't join us at the table but sat on a coffer beside the fire, sipping sparingly from the wine. When the last of the pudding had been cleared away and the cheese, nuts and brandy placed on the board, she turned to Richard with a smile.

"I confess to a most ill-bred curiosity about your escape from your Uncle Richard. Everyone thought you'd perished at his hand," she said softly apologetic.

Richard sighed and drew a deep breath, pushing his hanap away. His hair glowed gilt, and his smoke-blue eyes were violet shadowed in the firelight. I thought him wondrously handsome.

"It was like a miracle, Lady," he said bleakly. "God heard my prayers and delivered me from my tormentors.

"As you know, my brother and I had been lodged in the royal apartment of the Tower to prepare for his coronation. But our uncle, manufacturing some tale of our father having been married to the Lady Eleanor Butler before he married our mother, thus rendering us children all illegitimate and therefore ineligible to rule, took the throne himself.

"He hustled us out of the royal apartments and put us in mean confinement nearby."

He frowned as if in bitter remembrance and flexed his extended hands. "We . . . my brother and I, had drifted off to sleep the night of August 1 when two men . . . I had only the impression of them being big and smelling of ale . . . brought us abruptly awake by whipping cords around our wrists. Frail as we were and startled so, they had no trouble having us bound and gagged in moments.

"My brother, who had been suffering with an affliction of the jaw—indeed, always having been ailing—fainted away and was like a sack thrown over the shoulder of the bigger of the two. I fought and wiggled furiously, and my captor, cursing, fetched me a strong clout alongside my ear that forced me to subside a bit.

"They took us to a spot in the cellars below us to a tiny niche in the foundation walls. I saw that there were building materials lying hard by. They thrust us within and promptly *walled us up.*"

Mother blanched but made no comment. I, of course, had heard the story before and it filled me with the same deep horror as did the first telling. I stared at Richard. There was a fine dew of perspiration across the well-formed lip, and his hands kept flexing convulsively on the board.

"They went away very quickly, leaving us to the deepest, most helpless silence I've ever known. I managed to wriggle loose from my bounds; indeed, I think they'd disdained to secure them well, feeling that, even if we freed ourselves, we'd soon die from lack of air in our dark tomb. I groped about until I found my brother's face and pulled the cloth away from it. But he had already stopped breathing. I . . . I . . . thank God that he hadn't regained consciousness before he died.

"I began to shout and tear at the walls," he continued, "until my hands were bloodied and I'd lost a nail." He held his left hand up, showing us that the index finger had, indeed, lost a fingernail. It had healed over with skin, puckered and white, but there was no sign of the fingernail. "Finally, weakened and dizzy, realizing that I, too, would die, more agonizingly than my poor brother, I lay down beside him, gathered him into my arms, and tried to pray for courage.

"Then, unbelievably, I heard someone calling softly and scratching at the newly cemented wall. I sat up and pulled myself close to it, crying out to let whoever it was know that I was there and still alive.

"My rescuer attacked the wall with a bar or something else that clanged . . . later, I saw that it was a pike and, in a moment, had pulled out a great stone. A shaft of light pierced the dark hole and I lunged toward it, gulping deeply.

"Sir Robert Brakenbury, the Governor of the Tower, both in Father's reign and Uncle Richard's, was kneeling there, grasping at the edge of the other stones, tears coursing down his cheeks.

" 'Thank God, oh, thank God and Saint Mary,' he kept crying, reaching forward to touch my face and head as if to assure himself I was truly alive. 'And your brother, Your Grace?'

"I told him Edward was dead.

"He attacked the wall furiously, making a hole large enough to draw me through, explaining as he did that when the ruffians had come to the Tower with orders signed by my Uncle Richard to take us away, he'd shown them our little room, then, fearing for our safety, watched from concealment, intending to follow the men when they left. If they'd indeed taken us to our uncle, he planned, he said, to protest such wild and low-born men being sent for us and, if they'd attempted any mayhem on our persons, he'd have interfered, though likely it would have meant his own disgrace and death. Then, when he saw their intention, he realized that if he but kept quiet until they'd left, he'd have time to rescue us and get us away safely and Richard would never know we'd escaped."

He stared into the fire and tears formed in the magnificent eyes. "It was a fair plan on such short notice. Only poor Ned, my brother and king, didn't live long enough to be rescued.

"We walled my brother back up, for there was nothing to be gained from taking him out and risking discovery. Sir Robert took me away to Dover secretly and paid a Portuguese captain to take me on as a cabin boy. Told him some tale of me being his new wife's child and liable to inherit her fine inn someday. He gave me money beforehand, sewn secretly within my clothes, and when I reached the Continent I was able to survive and find Sir John, who'd fled England after Bosworth."

"A thrilling tale, lad," Father said a bit dryly. "By the rood, you could make your living telling it in castles and halls all over Ireland."

Richard flushed, and I could have cheerfully kicked Father.

"It's all true, milord," Richard said stiffly.

"I can verify that," Sir John said, bluff and hearty. "I swear the lad knows things only a royal prince could know of King Edward's household."

"*You* were a member of King Edward's household, milord," Father drawled. "The lad could have been coached."

"Father! How can you speak so?" I cried, "Ah, I have been sitting here in wonder and pity, watching the agony of the retelling . . ."

Father sighed in exasperation, then reached out and patted my outflung hand. "Magheen, darling, I've not your reasons for wanting to believe him," he said. "Nor am I saying, definitely, that I don't. But crowning the organmaker's son cost me . . . . and Ireland dear. I'll not be chasing a will-o'-the-wisp again. I'll need more proof than such a tale."

I opened my mouth to protest further, but Mother intervened.

"Not another word, Margaret," she said soothingly. "You can't expect more from your father than that. Nor can you, milords," she added, smiling at Richard and Sir John.

"Indeed, no, milady," Sir John said smoothly. "Your gracious invitation to Maynooth is all we could ask of you. In time, I know His Royal Grace will convince you."

Alice, as if having been waiting for a break in the conversation, tugged Father's sleeve.

"Sire, Cormac O'Connor's come. May we not call him in?"

Father smiled delightedly at the diversion. Cormac was a traveling bard who customarily spent the time from Saint Nicholas Day to Twelfth Night with us, which he explained to the guests, adding to Alice that we would indeed welcome Cormac's entertainment.

"He knows all of Irish history," Mother said by way of explanation to Richard, "and many a fine song about Queen Deirdre and her sorrows, Maeve, or the crystal boat that carried Conla to Paradise."

"Who wants to hear that namby-pamby stuff," Alice scoffed, rubbing at a dirty spot on the back of her hand. "I'd far rather hear of the exploits of the Fionn and Fian. Now, *there* were soldiers!" she added with a quick glance at Richard.

Mother signed to one of the pages near the buttery screen and, in a few minutes, Cormac, handsome and faintly supercilious and wearing his lute about his neck, suspended from a silver cord which gleamed against his murrey doublet, strode into the hall.

"'Tis good to see you, Cormac," Father said, extending his hand to the minstrel.

"Glad to be here. Sorry, Gerait More, that you weren't back in time to break bread with us."

Walter Delahide frowned from across the table. He was

forever scolding Father and Mother about their liberality to the vast retinues of every poet and bard in Ireland who chanced our way.

"You'd think *him* the host and Gerait the guest," he muttered.

Cormac ignored him.

"You want to hear of the Fionn, Lady Alice?"

"Oh, aye."

But Mother protested. "Oh, Cormac, I think we should consult our guests' preference."

Richard glanced at Alice, his eyes twinkling. "I'd like to hear of this fine army myself," he said. "What is it that makes it so remarkable?"

Alice rose to the bait.

"Why, never was it known for a Fionn to act less than nobly. Even to be considered, a man had first to master twelve books of poetry, be able to protect himself with nothing but a hazel switch and shield from at least nine opponents while standing knee-deep in a trench, be able to escape pursuers in a deep wood by running without letting even his braid come unloosed or disturbing a branch or leaf, pluck a thorn from his foot in flight, and his vows of chivalry commanded him to choose his wife without portion, for her manners and virtues alone, to be gentle to all women and not to take anything for himself that another stood in need of, as well as to fight be the odds nine to one."

"Remarkable," said Richard, throwing me an enigmatic smile. "I especially like the part about choosing one's wife without regard for aught but her virtues."

My heart almost stood still. Why had he singled me out with that smoky-blue gaze? Oh, I *knew* he cared for me too. I knew it.

"Sing what the poet Oisin said of them to Saint Patrick, Cormac," Alice said.

Cormac grinned wickedly. "Are you sure you'd rather not sing it yourself?" he said sarcastically.

"Sing, Cormac," Alice commanded, clambering up on Father's lap.

Cormac picked up his lute good-naturedly, cocking a jaunty dark eyebrow at Alice.

He finished with a flourish of melody. Father, as usual, sentimentally moved as if he were Alice, smiled and blinked.

"Ah, Father," I cried, shrewdly, "that is true chivalry; to espouse the truth even if it be the cause of an underdog."

Father laughed good-humoredly. "Save your wheedling, miss. I told you I'd not be going to war in your behalf unless I'm convinced."

Before I could answer him, there was a hammering at the hall door. Michael, rousing himself from a doze beside the fire, ran to open it.

Piers Butler, his face a thundercloud, stood in the opening.

"You've done it this time, Kildare," he snapped, pulling his hat off in a flurry of snow. He strode into the hall, kicking the door shut behind him. "By the rood, it'll be God's own wonder if the king doesn't give you permanent lodging in the Tower. I warned you, God knows. And this time, because I've promised to marry into your family, I'm tarred with the same traitor's brush."

He strode across the hall to where we sat, open-mouthed, watching his progress.

"Sir Piers, what's amiss," Mother cried, the first of us to find her voice.

He bowed the slightest of bows toward her, slapping his hat against his leg.

"I've come as friend, Lady . . . Milord Gerait, you must take that on faith, though, if I had any sense, I'd hie me off to England to rescue my own affairs and leave you to your fate."

"By Saint Bride, I don't know what you're talking about," Father cried, rising. "I've done nothing except invite this lad here for Christmas. Believe me, he's not convinced me I should in any way risk the king's ire by backing him. You may tell your master I'm giving him no aid and, after a genial Christmas visit, he'll be on his way elsewhere."

"It's too late for that, Kildare. I warned you to send him packing when he first arrived. You well knew my cousin was off to England. When will you learn you can't play the king in Ireland? King Henry has James's account of all that's going on here, and you can be damned sure it isn't favorable to you."

"Who'd believe that false bastard?" Father sniffed.

"Henry will. He has."

"But I've promised Magheen to you as the king wished. He should know my word's my bond," Father said righteously.

"Aye, your word's your bond," Piers replied curtly. "But that doesn't prevent your extending the best hospitality of your house to these pretend boys. God, you even crowned Simnel. The king was right when he said you crazy Irish would crown apes at last."

"That was a subtle warning to *me*," Father said levelly, "and unnecessary it was. My heraldic device being the ape. Never have I given any king of England reason to suspect me of trying to set myself up in his place."

"Be that as it may, you've goaded him too far by entertaining this boy. The king has proof that he's no more the Duke of York than I am. His name is Perkin Warbeck and he's the son of a tax collector and boatman from Tournai."

Richard had sat silently through the entire exchange, but at the mention of the name he jumped to his feet and went to stand before the fire, back to us.

Father stared at the slender back speculatively. "So?" he said slowly.

"Father, you've only his word of that," I cried.

Piers fixed me with his black, angry eyes, a cynical smile playing across his mobile mouth.

"The retainer I trust most in my entire household has

brought me the word directly from Westminster. My trou-blemaking cousin hurried straight to the king and filled his ears with tales of intrigues between your father and this pretender. He says they plot to invade England with a force greater than the German mercenary army that in-vaded under the Simnel lad. He accused Baron Portlester of gross embezzlement of funds to finance it, using his post as treasurer of Ireland to do it."

Father came roaring out of his seat at that, and the words he used to describe Black James turned the air in the hall blue and crackling.

"Milord Father never stole a grain o' salt in all his years —forty of them—as treasurer, and that black bastard well knows it. How can this Tudor king of yours be stupid enough to believe it?"

Piers laughed cynically.

"You can't be too surprised that he believes ill of you Geraldines when a skillful liar like my cousin maligns you. But I am drawn into the trap he's laid for you, I fear. We Butlers are *English!* No one can call us other. We've all been educated . . . for several generations . . . right in the household of the kings of England. And yet, James has convinced His Grace that I, too, am a traitor. He has talked the king into giving him *my* post as Uncle Thomas' administrator of the Ormonde estates."

"No, I don't believe that; you're but diddling me, lad," Father muttered. "Why would he betray his own cousin?"

"Because *he* would like to be the next Earl of Ormonde. He and the Archbishop of Dublin have been planning to have his illegitimacy removed by law—and, so, the im-pediment to his inheriting. And"—here he stared long at me—"he's asked the king to give him your daughter Mar-garet as wife instead of to me."

"I'd kill him first," I hissed. "The vile liar."

Mother had risen shakily and come to put her arm around me.

"Then we must prove your goodwill and obedience to

the king and thwart this evil man by arranging for you and Margaret to be married at once, Sir Piers," she said determinedly.

"Mother, I don't want to marry him either," I wailed.

"You have no choice, Lady Margaret," was Piers's cold rejoinder. "I sent Sir James White to Westminster on the same packet that carried my cousin. He came away without stopping to pack to let me know how matters stand in England. Believe me, it's as bad as it can be. If you don't want to see your father attainted, arrested for treason, you'll do as your mother says. It's the only way we can prove we mean to obey the king's wishes. Your father's in grave danger of being removed as deputy and your grandfather as treasurer of Ireland. Believe me, my cousin means to have it all. Not only the Earldom of Ormonde but the Deputyship of Ireland too. Jimmy White says that when he left the king was about to sign an order for Black James and Sir Thomas Garth to head an army against the Pale, which means your father and grandfather. I see no way to forestall your father's complete ruin except for us to marry at once."

My eyes, swimming with tears, were on Richard's silent and eloquent figure. He didn't move a muscle to protest, but stood, back to us, staring into the fire. At last the priest, his mentor, Sir John Taylor, turned to Father with a sigh.

"I see there is no use seeking aid from *you*, milord," he said shortly.

"In God's truth, I never promised it," Father said defensively.

"But, Father, if he's Richard of York . . ." I began.

"Lady Margaret, are you stupid?" Piers snapped. "I have told you the king has proof he is not."

"The king seems to have proof of just what he wants to believe," I said furiously.

Richard turned around at last.

"My dear Gerait More," he said almost conversationally, "I would not have you jeopardize your welfare because of me. I have had some contact with a representative of the French king, who has invited me to his court. I think, perhaps, I'll not stay with you at Maynooth for Christmas after all, but go on to France."

"Your decision couldn't possibly have something to do with what I've told you about Sir James Butler and his army being almost on my heels, could it?" Piers said contemptuously.

Richard flushed and, instead of answering, turned to his people with instructions for gathering baggage and horses to return to Dublin, where they'd find a ship to France.

I hated Piers with all my heart.

Yet, down in the quiet, secret part of my heart, I knew that Richard was not the Duke of York. And if he was not, then he too was a liar as much as Sir James Butler. And, smitten though I was with him, I knew the one thing on earth I couldn't abide was a liar.

Without another word to any of them, I turned on my heel and went up to my room.

Richard . . . or Perkin Warbeck . . . and his retinue returned to Dublin and the first ship to leave Ireland that very night.

I realized that I'd built a great fantasy around him. I had wanted to believe, with all my heart and soul, that he was Richard of York, and I'd nearly convinced myself that he was.

Yet, pusillanimous clerk of a king that he was, Henry Tudor never said anything that he wasn't prepared to prove beyond a shadow of a doubt, and if he said Richard was the son of a Tournai boatman, the world could be certain he had proof of it. Nor had Richard made the slightest move to protest when Piers accused him of being a pretender.

Ah, but he'd been winsome. The fair young knight of my dreams. Yet, it had been what he represented more than his person that had appealed to me. He was a way to escape marrying against my will. Like a young child, I'd built up a storybook romance in my heart, and he'd betrayed my dreams. I was disappointed, resentful, and, if the truth were to be fully stated, a bit contemptuous. Never had the day dawned in Ireland when a *Fitzgerald* would have bided so peacefully had his rights been usurped! If he were a Plantagenet he was a poor shadow of what they had been, and so, then, perhaps England was better off without them.

So I comforted myself throughout the bitter night.

There was nothing to be done but to marry Piers, as the king bade. The thought that the king was foolish enough to listen to the troublemaking James filled me with apprehension. Could the man truly convince the king that *he* should be legitimized and made Earl of Ormonde in Piers's place? That *he* should marry me? Impossible as it seemed, the Tudor king had shown himself amenable to listening to the black liar. Perhaps he was only wily enough to use him as a deterrent to Father. But to accuse Grandfather FitzEustace of embezzlement! Any king who'd even pretend to believe such a tale was dangerous.

The conclusions I thus reached tended to subdue and steady me. For the good of my family and Ireland, which needed Father's firm, just rule, and to avoid being given in marriage to the odious James, there was nothing for me to do but to marry Piers as quickly as arrangements could be made.

We heard Mass the following morning, Saint Nicholas Day, in the chapel at Maynooth. As was the custom, Michael, Mother's page, assumed the role of the saint/bishop and read the sermon at Mass, being well rewarded by Father afterward. Michael, full of himself in tawdry bishop's robes and tarnished gilt miter, afterward brought me a message from Piers, who requested I speak to him in the library after breakfast.

There was no use refusing, I told myself grimly. I had worked through my despair the night before. I was to marry Piers, and there would be no Plantagenet prince on a fine white charger to save me. Grudgingly, I admitted to myself that he *had*, after all, come to warn us rather than run away to England to redeem himself in the king's eyes. That had shown a modicum of goodwill. So it was in a spirit of reason that I went to him in the library.

"There's hope for you yet," he said by way of greeting. "I am glad you saw the wisdom of talking with me."

I shrugged. "Why not? It seems we must accept this situation. I do understand that you probably never expected to marry a Fitzgerald any more than I expected to marry a Butler."

He nodded approvingly. "I'm glad you have come to that conclusion. It is always easier to discuss matters with a reasonable individual than a wild little firebrand."

I let that pass, although his controlled manner tended to set my teeth on edge.

"Since neither of us has the slightest choice in this matter," he continued, "it seems requisite that we make the best of it."

"That is what I am trying to do."

"I would like to say, Lady Margaret, that in spite of my family's differences over the years with yours, there is no doubt at all in my mind that my cousin's wild accusations against your father and grandfather are false. For all Baron Portlester's dreamy romanticism and lack of business sense, no one can seriously believe he ever embezzled money from Ireland. Even Diogenes would have had to admit he'd found an honest man in him. As to your father, while he's certain to be in the center of any wild foolishness in Ireland, he, too, is an honest man according to his lights, and Henry won't condemn him for being pro-Yorkist."

I nodded in grudging thanks for his faith in my father and grandfather. "It's too bad *you* don't have the king's ear instead of your vile cousin," I ventured.

"That would be desirable, but since I do not, we must just show the king by our actions that we mean to do his will. In time, I believe, Henry will come to see my cousin for the self-server and liar that he is."

"In the meantime, my father is in danger of being attainted for treason."

"I believe he himself can best resolve that problem, Lady Margaret, and it's partly for this that I wanted to talk to you. You must try to make him see that, while Henry is not the most personable king ever to sit at Westminster, he is the only qualified one we have. Indeed, he has tried his best to please and understand Yorkist feelings, too, by marrying Elizabeth of York. He is conscientious and sensible and he means to make England a world power . . . respected throughout the world. Your father can follow him with a clear heart, knowing that serving this new king of ours is serving Ireland best."

What he said made sense. Indeed, to give Henry his due, he'd exacted no harsh penalties after Bosworth. Father and the other barons angrily decried the document he'd issued making himself king the day *before* Bosworth, and thus, making all those who'd fought on King Richard's side traitors. But he'd done it only to establish that he *was* king as the Lancastrian heir. He'd promptly removed all the attainders immediately if the men involved would swear fealty to him. He'd announced his intention of marrying Edward's oldest daughter and behaved with great restraint to all. Some of the Yorkists had fled England after the battle, but even any of those who made submission to his rule were welcomed back and restored to their estates. I knew that Piers's assessment of Henry's character was right. Slowly, I nodded agreement.

"I will do what I can, of course, to make Father see the wisdom of what you say."

"Good. Sensible lass. I knew no daughter of Gerait More could be other than courageous and intelligent. I'm glad you are also reasonable. We should have a fine, sensible marriage."

I smiled wryly. "Sensible" was not the adjective I would have chosen to describe the marriage I wanted. As if he read my mind, he smiled too.

"That is not to your liking, Lady Margaret? Of course, I

realize, you'd prefer to be swept off your feet by the likes of your pretty pretender. Often, marriages that start so end with the fine knight beating his wife, seeking to keep her from her family and friends, installing his mistresses in the castle village, or dissipating her dower lands. Would you like something like that?"

"Of course not," I said, laughing in annoyance. "But . . ."

"But . . . you'd like a bit of romance as well," he finished. "Well, my dear Lady Margaret, perhaps I can satisfy your thwarted desires along that line as well." Before I realized what he was about, he'd pulled me into his arms, one hand behind my neck, entangling itself in my hair, forcing my lips to meet his. He drew me tightly against him, lip to lip, breast to chest, the hard column of his body setting up a wild, unaccustomed clamor in my heart. There was nothing sensible about it! The strong, almost painful, yet infinitely tender, pressure of his long fingers across the back of my head and his thumb lifting my chin to his kiss, the hot demanding lips of him, his arms, imprisoning and lifting me, filled me with startling, sudden rapture. I gasped and threw my arms around him, kissing him back, pressing against him. We clung together for a timeless moment, and when we parted it was he who moved first. He laughed in triumph.

"By the rood, I knew you'd respond like that. Such a woman fate has given me . . ."

Shakily, I stared up into the gloating brown eyes. How could I have been so wanton? What kind of girl was I to act so with a man I didn't love—indeed, a man all reason bid me to hate?

"How dare you?" I cried, feeling my face turning scarlet. I stumbled out of his embrace, wiping furiously at my mouth like a child who's tasted something bad.

For a moment, something almost like apology flitted across his face, but was gone so quickly I thought I'd imagined it. He was laughing, mocking as usual. He made a quick gesture, as if the kiss had been of no consequence.

"As I said, Lady Margaret," he said ironically, "we might as well make the best of it."

I hated him with all my heart. Now he had my wild response to mock me with. I would show him. Never again would that happen. I would steel myself against him. Marry him I must, but no one mocked Margaret Fitzgerald. Too furious to speak, I whirled around and ran from the library.

Eleanor had been betrothed to her Calvagh O'Connor Faly the same day I had been betrothed to Piers. They were to wait a year since Calvagh, the tanist of his family now that his older brother, Toirdelbach, had died, was being taught all he'd need to know of governing the family lands. Like Alice's Fian, he was also much involved in warfare, for there was usually some disagreement beyond the Pale among the families.

How I wished that I was marrying a man of my choice, as she was! She confided happily that she'd loved Calvagh since he'd come with his father to Saint Thomas Court several years before, but she'd not been able to get him to ask Father for her hand, he being too proud to ask for a great heiress when he was but a younger son with little lands and no title to come to him. The death of his brother had changed that.

It had also saved Eleanor from being the one to marry a Butler. Though, in God's truth, I could not have found it in my heart to have wanted her to when she obviously loved her O'Connor Faly so much.

Margaret the martyr, I called myself, bitterly mocking. I was delivering myself up for my family and country. But I was not doing it with saint-like resignation. I would obey the letter of King Henry's law but not its spirit. Piers's mocking eyes when I'd kissed him so shamelessly haunted me. Always, when we chanced to meet, his eyes laughed at me, sharing the memory, and I writhed in humiliation. Oh, I'd make him pay. He would never possess me.

Mother and her women sewed night and day on the fabric Piers had brought from Waterford. We were to be married on Saint Stephen's Day, first after Christmas. As I stood before Mother's long brass mirror-disk for fittings, I knew the gown was becoming. The silkiness of it lay gently across breast and hip, and the green hue of it made my eyes look like haunted fairy wells in deep shade.

The day came too soon.

Father had ordered the Archbishop of Dublin, the abrasive Walter Fitzsimmonds, to perform the ceremony, as if to mock his sympathy to legitimizing Black James. Indeed, after the ceremony, before he'd even kissed me in congratulation, he fixed the belligerent prelate with his fierce blue gaze and said, "Take news of *this* to Westminster, Your Grace!"

I stood frozen beside Piers, accepting the good wishes of the family, all our own as well as those of Father's able to attend, Uncle Thomas' widow, Uncle Jimmy and his wife and little ones, Aunt Eleanor with her husband, big Conn More O'Neill and their small, wild son, and Mother's only brother, quiet Uncle Thomas FitzEustace, his wife, Margaret, newly married themselves. Our castle people, too, kissed me, wishing me well.

Yet, despite the Christmas cheer and the congenial assembly, my heart was as bleak and cold as the rain that slashed the walls of Maynooth. Mother, nearly ready to take to childbed now, had still managed to provide a sumptuous feast, and soon the great hall was noisy with laughter and many a proffered toast to Piers and me. I sat, unsmiling, feeling I'd done my duty and unwilling to pretend to like it, dreading the time when I'd be alone with the man who was my husband.

I would not succumb to him, I vowed.

We stayed in the hall longer than usual, neither Piers nor I being willing to be the first to give the sign to retire. He kept drinking steadily, responding to every toast with one of his own, so that my family thought him affable.

I thought him despicable. Like as not he'd be drunk as well as demanding. Still, he did not signal me to retire.

Finally, Mother, seeing the way it was, came to lead me away to bed, as was the custom. I could see that my white silence pained and troubled her, but I could not find it in my heart to be concerned with her feelings. I'd done what they wanted; if their consciences hurt, so be it.

But as she put the candle on the bedside table and leaned over to kiss me, I had to relent. She was so sad and lovely, so weary with the great mound that marred her slender, delicate form, and I knew she could not have done anything about my dilemma.

I put my arms around her neck and held her for a moment. "It's all right, Mamma," I said, using the old childhood name, "I'll be all right. Go to bed; you're dropping on your feet."

She smiled dazzlingly and the weariness seemed to disappear. It was as though she accepted my caress and reassuring words as absolution. "God bless you, Magheen," she whispered. "I pray you'll come to love him as I love your father." She gave me one last hug and left, taking her women with her.

Tears stung my eyes. I knew her prayer could never come true. How I'd longed for a man I could love, almost worship, as she did Father.

And I'd gotten Piers Butler.

He didn't come for two hours. I feigned sleep although I'd been lying awake beside the guttering candle, relieved yet furious that he showed his contempt by staying away. He'd thought to find me languishing for his embrace, had he? Resolutely, I kept my eyes tightly shut, turned with my back to the center of the great bed.

He didn't attempt to get into bed with me. I heard him walk to the side of the bed and stop. I breathed evenly, feigning sleep, but he was not deceived. He laughed mockingly. To have pretended any further would have been ridiculous. I opened my eyes and stared at him. He wore a loose, soft robe of crimson and his face was shadowed, mysterious in the firelight. He seemed to sway a little and I saw his sardonic smile, yet his eyes were hidden from me.

"You're drunk," I said contemptuously.

"Aye, but only enough to . . . make things interesting."

"You're disgusting."

"You didn't think so the other day."

Swiftly he leaned forward and pulled me into his arms. Unbidden, indeed, ignoring my heart's commands to stop, my body began its wild clamor at the sight and smell and feel of him. I was filled with loathing for myself! Was I a mare in heat to so want the embrace of a man that I'd burn for a Butler?

I rolled away. He'd not kiss me, for then I'd be lost. I pushed at him, scrambling to the other side of the bed, escaping for the moment as he righted himself.

"Leave me alone," I cried. "If you had any decency, you'd know I hated you and you'd leave me alone."

He stared at me enigmatically. At last he laughed.

"I'm not the man to have to ravish a maid," he drawled. "There are too many willing to have Piers Butler make love to them for that."

He pulled his robe about him and walked toward the door, turning just before he left the room.

"I could take you, Margaret," he said softly. The candle sputtered and went out, and the fire, disturbed by the draft from the open door, flared up to light his dark eyes.

"I just don't think it would be worth the effort," he said deliberately as he shut the door behind him.

I never knew where he spent our wedding night.

CHAPTER 4

The following day Mother gave birth to a daughter, whom she named Eustacia for Grandfather FitzEustace, much to his delight.

I was deeply relieved that her ordeal should have been over before Piers and I had to go to Kilkenny, for, though Sir James had usurped his post as deputy to the Earl of Ormonde, he could hardly put him out of the castle that had been his home, when in Ireland, all his life.

She called me to her room shortly after the birth and asked that Piers and I stand godparents to my baby sister. I knew that she was attempting to establish us, in my mind, as a couple, and so, though I felt I'd hate him forever, I could not refuse her.

At least Piers had been discreet enough that no one in the castle seemed to realize our marriage had not been consummated. For that, at least, I was grateful to him, for it was a humiliation to me that he'd walked out on me, although I'd have been put on the rack before I'd have admitted it to him. And when I asked him to stand godfather to the baby, he accepted agreeably enough.

Indeed, he'd seemed delighted with little Eustacia, who promised to be beautiful. Father came across the great hall with the baby in his arms, all the little ones in his wake, the evening she was born. He was smiling proudly.

Walter, seeing to the clearing of the board, stared at the baby glumly.

"Too bad she wasn't another lad, Gerait," he said.

"What need have I of another lad?" Father said, not to be baited with a beautiful new child in his arms. Always he had been transported with joy when his children were born, though only Gerry was the boy needful as heir to the honor of Kildare. "Gerry's lad enough, and Ireland has need of such grace and beauty as this."

"May I hold her, milord?" Piers said suddenly. I stared at him in some surprise; I would not have thought him eager to hold a baby.

Father shifted her carefully from his arms to Piers, helping my husband to accommodate his arms to the tiny bundle. "Mark you, Son-in-law, they quite often baptize a man in their own way. I've been so done to by all these pretty scamps," he said.

The children laughed naughtily at the notion of having so discomfited Father. They clambered around Piers to see the baby.

"You'd think they'd never seen a baby before," Walter said in disgust.

"We'll have the christening in the morning, for, by Saint Bride, even Christmas has not served to deter your cousin and Thomas Garth from their depredations. Now that the Lady Allison is delivered, I'll be riding out. I've kept Walter Fitzsimmonds here to baptize the child," Father said. "Here, you'd best give her to me; when they start fidgeting and working their mouths that way, you'll learn in time it means they're looking for their mother's breast again."

Piers relinquished the baby almost reluctantly. His dark eyes glowed soft as he stared down at her. It was a facet of his character I had not anticipated, and it softened me toward him somehow. For, though Father had always been tenderhearted about his babes, I knew most men were not. Or at least were ashamed to let anyone know if they were.

When Father had started toward Mother's room, shooing the children away, Piers turned to us uncertainly.

"I confess, I know nothing of being a godfather," he said. "Could one of you instruct me?"

Alice, who loved babies and never missed a christening among the villagers, pounced on that.

"Oh, aye, Sir Piers, there's nothing I can't tell you. Come

along to the chapel. Elizabeth, you and Gerry go to the nursery for a doll."

The children ran off to do as she bid and soon joined us in the chapel, for, while I would have not gone with the rest, Alice insisted I, as godmother, must hold the "baby."

Alice thrust the doll at me and drew herself up beside the baptismal font, puffing out her cheeks and glaring down her nose in a remarkably accurate imitation of Archbishop Fitzsimmonds.

"Bring forth the little bundle of woe, so sadly stained by Satan's curse," she intoned, folding her arms across her little, thrust-out belly in the exact way the archbishop folded his across his paunch.

Piers burst out laughing, and I lowered my head over the doll to hide my own amusement. Alice warmed to his appreciation.

"While I have this opportunity," she intoned, still in her idea of the archbishop's voice, "I shall attempt to point out to you your great wickedness and perfidy, you poor, sniveling Butler. Do you think to escape the yawning jaws of hell? You with your hidden lecheries and thievery. Only the gracious blood of the Lamb can save you from hell."

Elizabeth giggled outright. "Child, cease that uproar. It isn't seemly in the house of God," Alice roared.

I began to think her behavior wasn't seemly, however funny it was. "Alice, enough of that," I said sternly. "Just show Sir Piers what will be done and where he'll have to respond."

She threw me a look of resignation, but dared one last bit of clowning.

"Now, then, Sir Godfather," she said, "come and lay your hand on this sin-stained babe, for I must hurry with the christening. I feel a great need of refreshing myself with a tun of wine."

Piers was hard put to keep a seemly face throughout the rehearsal, and next day, as the archbishop of Dublin read the sacred rite, he seemed in constant danger of laughing aloud, for Alice had done a perfect imitation of the archbishop's pompous, overbearing manner. I kept my head studiously lowered throughout, not daring to meet his eyes, or we'd have disgraced ourselves at once.

Oddly, the strained camaraderie disturbed me. There was so much about Piers Butler that I liked. He had the same wild, irreverent mind of the Fitzgeralds, quick to see humor in pomposity. Already my little brother and sisters adored him, although he did nothing to woo their favor, and they, like I, had heard little good of Butlers from their cradles.

But he had humiliated me, scorned me. And after himself hurrying to Maynooth to urge our marriage.

Since our wedding night he'd not returned to our room, and where he stayed I had no idea. Nor did anyone else seem to. Everyone assumed we shared a room; the men-at-arms made rough, teasing remarks to him. At least he spared me the humiliation of having the entire castle know he didn't sleep with me.

We were to go to Kilkenny after Twelfth Night and, as the days went by, I became acutely aware of how much I'd miss my family and the noisy, rough love we gave each other. If I'd been going in the company of a man I loved, it would have been a poignant but happy experience; as it was, I was devastated. My life seemed to stretch off ahead of me desolately and interminably.

Even Christmas had not stopped the raids by Sir James's and Sir Thomas Garth's army. The king had authorized it, but he couldn't know how the two commanders abused their privilege. No reasonable man would have loosed such monsters knowingly. They were to "preserve the peace" in Ireland. The truth was that they rode hard, raiding, burning, raping and looting. There was hardly a day when Father didn't ride out to put down some insurrection Sir James's men had caused in the first place. Indeed, long before Twelfth Night, Father had been forced to go back to Saint Thomas Court to muster the Guild leaving Mother and the children at Maynooth. Piers and I with his retinue which was too small for safety against the notorious "army"

Sir James and Sir Thomas were leading, took the opportunity to ride along as far as Dublin, where more of the
Kilkenny people were to join us as escort the rest of the
way.

Father had, of course, sent off a courier to England with
news of our marriage and to protest to the king the lawless
acts of the commanders of his army. Moreover, he'd sent
heralds throughout Ireland, assuring them of the protection of the Guild as long as he was Deputy Lord of the
Palace and stating in no uncertain terms that Sir James
Butler was without the law to be using the king's army to
raid and steal and rape.

It was not surprising, therefore, that we'd scarcely
reached Dublin when a messenger in the livery of the king
came from Sir James Butler saying he, Sir James, was coming to Dublin "to clear himself of slanders."

Of course, when Father heard that, the walls of Saint
Thomas reverberated with his roars. Having vented the
worst of his rage, he strode through the palace, issuing
sharp orders for armor to be shined, spears to be sharp-
ened, even the six muskets, Father's pride, that had come
as a gift from Madam Margaret of Burgundy as a New
Year's gift three years before and issued to the palace
guard, were to be cleaned and readied for action.

The following afternoon, the entire army arrived and
proceeded to set up camp on the grounds of the park
below Saint Thomas Court.

Father was livid. He went out himself and ordered them
off, one man, disdaining even a personal guard, standing
up to the king's entire army.

"He's mad," Piers said beside me as we watched from
the battlements. "Does he think he's God?"

"He's courageous," I snapped. "But I suppose a Butler
would consider a display of courage mad."

I knew I was behaving contentiously, but such was the
pattern our marriage seemed to be falling into. I resented
having to marry Piers, and even more, I resented that he

was so singularly detached. Most of the time he ignored my bursts of bad temper or smiled his superior smile. Today, however, my remark must have stung him, for he frowned and turned toward the inner stair.

"Of course, I would expect you to react that way. But, fool that he is, I expect he'll be needing help. You'd best not stay out here long; it's growing cold."

He clattered down the stairs.

Not wanting to miss anything, I followed him, thinking how like him it was to be concerned for my health even when he was angry with me. I suppose he wanted to make sure I lived long with him so he could enjoy my discomfiture the more, I thought peevishly. Nothing about our marriage seemed to be turning out the way I'd planned. I'd intended to make him miserable, make him suffer because he couldn't win me or my love. Yet, most of the time, he seemed unmiserable, entirely, and his lack of misery was humiliating.

Piers quickly gathered a guard and was on the point of going outside to back Father when the latter came in, calling for his armor and weapons.

"They're going to the abbey grounds, damned murdering outlaws," he said with grim satisfaction. "I've told Sir James I'll meet him in St. Patrick's nave. I'll be damned if I'll have them within the walls of Dublin."

"I'm going too," I said suddenly.

"The hell you are," Father cried.

"You can't stop me, Father, I'm married now," I said smugly. "There's one good thing to be said for it, anyhow."

"Piers won't let you go either, mizzy-mind," was the reply.

"I'd like to see him try to keep me home!"

Piers's dark eyes were snapping with malicious laughter. "Oh, I'm not the man to waste my strength on worthless causes," he laughed. "Besides, milord, there'll be little trouble with my cousin, I think, when he confronts you. You are, for the present, still deputy to the viceroy."

As usual, he'd avoided a direct confrontation with me; as usual, I was left with a sense of frustration and the knowledge I'd behaved like a spoiled child.

I hurried away for my cloak and to order my horse saddled. By the time the Guild had mustered, I was ready to ride out with them.

Father and Grandfather, Walter Delahide, Jimmy Boyce, and Lionel Howth went ahead of us into the church where Sir James, Sir Thomas Garth, and perhaps four others were waiting. The troops were assembled on the green outside, allowing us passage, then pushing in toward the church porch so as not to miss anything. For the first time I felt a stirring of fear, but, with Piers there behind me, I was determined not to show it. At least Father seemed unconcerned by the vastly greater numbers of the army outside. But I'd never known him to show fear of that sort. He knew who he was, Gerait More, head of all the Fitzgeralds, the greatest family in Ireland, and, moreover, deputy to the king's viceroy since his father's death when he was only twenty-one. In all those years he'd been ruler of Ireland in all but name. He had no fear of the likes of Sir James Butler.

"What mean you, bastard, by using the king's army as an excuse for your lechery and raping?" Father roared.

Sir James, resplendent in black armor, which he always affected, according to Piers, as a defiant exploitation of his nickname, laughed loudly, showing strong white teeth.

"You are charging me with *rape?* I who can have for the asking the loveliest women in Waterford town?"

"'Tis good you can beguile the Waterford trulls, for by Saint Bride, all the women of the Pale barricade their doors and say their beads not to fall into your hands when the word's out that you're coming."

Sir James flushed. "They but listen to your slanders. And suspicious they should be, too, of the likes of one who harbors low-life pretenders to His Highness' crown."

It was Father's turn to flush.

"I harbor no pretenders now. The lad the king calls

Warbeck is on his way to France. I have explained it all to His Grace. Moreover, my daughter Margaret has married Piers Butler, as the king commanded."

Sir James's head shot up at that. "I'd not yet heard that, Gerait More. I confess I'm disappointed that it's so. His Highness has made me temporary deputy to the Earl of Ormonde. He . . . thought my cousin Piers, too, was traitorous."

Piers's jaw worked angrily.

"What could have given him such a notion, pray, cousin?" he said sarcastically.

Sir James looked up the aisle to where we were standing. Catching sight of me, he grinned and bowed. "Ah, Lady Margaret, you should have waited, lass. I have great hopes of convincing the king to make my appointment permanent. It seems likely my illegitimacy will soon be reversed. I trow, *I* could please you better than my bookish cousin. But, of course, if my plans work out, an annulment can be arranged."

"You think I would marry you any more willingly than Piers?" I said in revulsion.

"By God, Magheen, don't even answer the worthless bastard," Father roared, charging toward Black James with sword drawn.

In seconds, the church was alive with flying arrows. They pierced the rood screen and stuck out like feathered ornaments from the saints' statues and occasionally even hit a man. With a muttered oath, Piers grabbed me roughly and thrust me into a pew, ordering me to keep down.

"Why did your father have to attack him?" he fumed. "I tell you, Margaret, he's mad. He's supplying fuel by the cartload for James's fire of gossip to the king."

"Shut up!" I hissed, peering up over the edge of the pew.

Father had reached Black James and grabbed him in his great arms, lifting him bodily off his feet.

"Lay down your arms," he roared. "By God, we're still within a church."

"Aye, good advice," said Sir James virtuously. "Belated though your recognizance of our whereabouts."

"Then, come outside, damn you." Father released him and pushed him ahead down the dim aisle. As they passed me, Sir James bowed mockingly in my direction, his black eyes raking me.

Piers swore softly and jerked me behind him.

"I wish you'd have stayed at home like a reasonable lass," he snapped, striding in Father's path. "You keep things stirred up abominably. Just like a Fitzgerald."

"It isn't a Fitzgerald who started this ruckus," was my angry retort, keeping in step with him.

Outside, the green of the quadrangle was swarming with people. There was much shouting and hand-to-hand combat, and I realized the citizens of Dublin had come out, quite spontaneously, to attack the army with pikes and clubs and even, in the case of some of the women, with chaffing pans. How gratifying it was to see, since, for the most part, the people of Meath had done little to help Father against the marauders.

Father's face split in a wide grin. We were no longer outnumbered, although the Dubliners were far inferior in arms. Still, at last someone was willing to repulse the lawless army and back up the Guild.

Sir James, however, looked stricken.

"Ah, you've a little less stomach for battle when the odds are more even," Father laughed grimly. "Come, then, what are these 'slanders' you accuse me of spreading?"

Sir James turned and dashed for the door of the chapter house across the quadrangle, which was, of course, a sanctuary. Grandfather FitzEustace, evidently reading his mind, as I had, and realizing that if he reached sanctuary he could not be touched for forty days, jumped forward to try to intercept him. Sir James knocked the old man, who was little better than half his size, flying against Lionel. He'd reached the chapter house door before Father, roaring with rage at the blow to Grandfather, reached him. The door slammed in Father's face.

Piers was as quick to reach my grandfather's side as I was.

"I'm all right," Grandfather cried, struggling up and forward to see what was happening. "Get the black villain, Gerald," he added with relish.

Father was hacking furiously at the heavy oaken door with his battle-ax. Soon he had a sizable hole.

"Kildare, you'd violate the holy sanctuary?" came Sir James's horrified voice from within.

Piers ran forward to stand at Father's side. "You can't do this, Milord Gerait," he said in a voice that echoed the horror in Sir James's. "No Christian knight can do such a vile thing."

"I'm not trying to drag him out," Father fumed. "I want only to talk to him, and words can't penetrate that heavy door."

I was not sure that such had been his intention, but if it had not, the exertion of hacking the hole had given Father time to gain control of his temper and he stepped back a little, thrusting the ax into his belt.

"Butler, I've got you now and you know it," he said sternly. "It occurs to me that the best thing I could do for Ireland would be to hang you right now. But as your cousin, here, points out, 'tis not the way of a Christian so to do. Now, entirely too much has been said on both sides, I can't deny, but you must admit that you've been the instigator of these troubles. My daughter's married to your cousin, as the king commanded, and is even now on her way to Kilkenny in his company to assume her place in his home. You have no reason, therefore, to accuse Sir Piers of treason any more than you've had reason to accuse me."

"That's funny, Kildare. Everything you've done in Ireland since Bosworth has been treasonable."

"I beg to differ with you and will convince the king of my good faith, I assure you," was the angry answer. "But let that pass for the moment and consider the two cases separately. It's a fact and a truth of God that my son-in-law has done nothing in the least treasonable, and you'll have to tell the king so even though it will mean you'll have to relinquish your new duties as deputy to the Earl of Ormonde."

There was heavy silence from within the chapter house.

"Is that agreeable to you?"

More silence.

"By God, Butler, I'll keep you in there until Gabriel blows his trumpet if you don't answer me!"

At last Sir James cleared his throat huskily.

"I'll agree to tell the king that Piers has married Margaret and has had nothing to do with your treasons," came the reply.

Father ignored the remark about himself. He nodded with satisfaction, flicking his blue eyes toward Piers, who smiled in spite of himself. I realized that being accused of treason when he'd been loyal to the king and worked hard to convince my father to follow suit must have been hard for Piers. And he *had* ridden out with the Guild against his own cousin.

. Father strode closer to the door.

"Now, then," he said, "I can see I've a deal of explaining to do to the king about my own loyalties, and that shall be between him and me with no interference from the likes of you. But now you must get yourself back to London to set things straight about my son-in-law. So, if you'll stick your hand through the hole in the door, I'll shake it in sign you may come out and depart in peace to set right the mischief you've caused."

"Nay, Kildare, I'll not stick forth my hand. You'd strike it off with your ax."

Father sighed deeply and his face took on a look of exasperation. "I'm not as treacherous as you, dog in a manger that you are," he said, "but I want this matter set to rights and you out of Ireland, so, here, take my hand on it." He thrust his arm through the hole in the door.

"Watch him, Gerald," Grandfather cried. "He who accuses another of ill faith is usually guilty of it himself. You'll lose *your* hand."

"If I do, by God, I'll choke the bloody bastard with the whole one," Father said grimly.

Sir James must have believed him for I saw his hand grasp Father's, and, when Father had withdrawn his hand, the chapter house door swung inward slowly and Sir James stood outlined in the doorway. He motioned to Thomas Garth, who brought his horse forward, and in a minute he'd mounted and rode slowly across the quadrangle toward the harbor, much to the delight of the Dubliners.

"Do you think he'll really return to England, Gerald?" Grandfather asked, staring after the armed band.

"He'd better," Father said. "But I've no way of forcing him to. Like as not, soon's the ship's out of the harbor, they'll sail south to Waterford."

"You'd best plan to go to England yourself, Gerald. 'Tis time to make your peace with the king, I think."

Father nodded reluctantly. "I'll go as soon as possible. But I can't leave the people of Meath to Black James's tender mercies. I'll have to be sure *he's* in England before I do."

"I'd advise you to avoid sheltering any more Simnels or Warbecks, milord," Piers said dryly.

Father threw him a look of annoyance. "I know how to conduct myself without any advice from you," he said.

We made our way back to Saint Thomas Court in stiff silence. I was more annoyed than Father at Piers presuming to judge him.

But in my heart I knew that he was right, and I prayed my father would have enough sense to listen to him. It seemed that it wouldn't take very much to have the king arrest him for treason.

Father didn't want us to go on to Kilkenny, unsure as he was of Black James's whereabouts, and Piers's castle being so close to Waterford, which had become James's headquarters. We were safe within the Pale, he argued. There was much room at Maynooth for us and Piers's people until a more propitious time to go south. He was, of course, concerned for our safety, but he hated to part with me too, I thought.

But Piers was adamant about resuming his duties at Kilkenny.

"The day's never dawned when I'd bide in safe retreat from my cousin James," he declared. "Besides, he'd not dare attack us. We have done the king's will; likely he knows of our wedding by now. Even James would not dare harm us."

Nonetheless, Father and the Guild rode south with us, leaving us two days later when we turned off the southern way for the last stage of the journey to Kilkenny. I sat my horse, watching them out of sight, then turned my palfrey toward Kilkenny.

I'll not cry! I'll not cry before this Butler and his men, I told myself, riding on with head held high. But Piers wasn't deceived. He urged his horse into step with mine.

"*Gloating?*" I said bitterly, although in my heart I didn't believe he was taking pleasure in my pain.

His lips tightened almost imperceptibly but he spoke calmly.

"Don't be like that, Margaret. I want you to know that I do understand what all this is costing you. I'll help you if I can."

"Thank you," I said grudgingly.

We rode in strained silence for a while. His men, glancing at each other and seeing the tears I couldn't hide, fell back as if to allow us privacy. Then Piers cleared his throat softly, an obvious preface to a remark, as I'd come to know.

"We've gotten off to a bad start, Margaret. I don't attempt to place any blame for it, but I do regret any part I may have had in it. We'll be at Kilkenny soon. It will be our home for the rest of our lives. It seems appropriate, to me at least, that we give a little thought to the fact. That we are joined together for better or worse. Doesn't it seem reasonable to you that we should make the best of it? What purpose does making each other miserable serve?"

"You will take the *reasonable* viewpoint no matter what," I said ironically.

"If that was meant as a criticism, I don't take it so. You can never insult me by accusing me of using reason. Reason. Logic. Deliberation before one acts. These qualities are all that separate man from the beasts. Men who indulge in temper outbursts, passion, histrionics . . . they're fools and worse. Such behavior makes them lower than animals."

"I suppose that's an indictment of me . . . my father too," I said with a strained laugh.

"At least your passions are not intrinsically evil, like my cousin's," he said complacently.

"I know that you're right," I conceded. "But, just as you win each argument, you convince me the more how different we two are. You *experience* life. I live it, *feel* it. You can say we ought to be sensible about this situation and make the best of it. It's in your nature to be made happy by the logical. Having no deep illogical feelings, you would be happy with any woman, provided she wasn't physically repulsive and was of a 'reasonable' nature. But I am a born romantic. I am the kind of woman you'd call a dreamer. I have always believed I'd be passionately in love with the man I married. I wanted to *adore* him and know that he reciprocated my feelings. How am I to live a lifetime with such as you? You are like . . . like . . . those new printing machines. You *know* that the words placed on each sheet of paper will be exact. It is impossible for them to be other than the plate that presses them."

He stared at me impassively.

"And if I am, Margaret, cannot you accept that?"

"I see that it would be best if I tried."

"Good lass. It's necessary that you do, I think. I feel that it's best . . ."

"You *feel* . . . ?" I laughed.

"You do right to correct me. I *think* it would be best if

our marriage were consummated. If a child were to be on the way, it would make Sir James's ridiculous talk of forcing through an annulment and marrying you less likely."

"Oh, I should have known you'd find a way to get to that, *reasonably*," I flared. "Your *reason* is always to your benefit."

"It would be to your benefit too. You'd be assured of safety from my cousin. And I might say, in all due modesty, there would be other benefits to you too."

"You'd use my loathing of your cousin, my fear of him, to get me to agree," I said resentfully.

"Are you afraid of him, Margaret?" he asked, not unkindly. "Don't be. I don't think Henry has any intention of replacing me permanently with my cousin. He's simply using him to harass your father into loyalty. But there's no use taking any chances."

"If you don't believe he'd replace you, then there is no need for our marriage to be consummated," I snapped. "You see, I can use your precious logic too."

"We are married, Margaret. It is the usual state of affairs for a husband and wife to be intimate, isn't it?"

"And shall we make an appointment?" I cried sarcastically. "Is there a logical time and place? Proper attire? Protocol to be followed?"

"You are needlessly upset by my seeming lack of ardor," he said. "I can assure you, I have strong physical desire and would not disappoint you."

"You're impossible," I cried. "I don't want to talk to you."

"I can't think why not. I am your husband and will be devoted to you."

"Because it's logical and sensible so to be?"

"Of course."

"I am not logical and sensible. I cannot accept . . . consummation of our marriage on those terms."

He sighed as if his patience was wearing thin. "Would you have me pretend lovesickness? Sing you ballads?

Pluck you a rose? That would certainly be impossible, the latter, in January."

"I can't think of anything more reprehensible to me," I said hotly. "I never thought I was so . . . unattractive that wooing me would require such sacrifice."

"You are certainly not unattractive. Is that what you want? Sweet talk?"

I began to laugh, almost hysterically. "Is that your idea of sweet talk? Heaven help the maid unfortunate enough to love you!"

He shook his head as if in bafflement.

"Margaret, I don't mean to insult you, but I must point out that more unfortunate yet would be the man who fell in love with *you*. You would tyrannize him worse than your late king, Richard III, did poor England."

"We seem to be agreed that we're equally unsuitable for falling in love with. But we're still unagreed upon conditions for . . . consummating a marriage."

"Until one or the other of us changes his mind, we seem to be stalemated, then."

"I believe that we are." I urged my horse on ahead of him, effectively ending the discussion. He didn't attempt to come up beside me, but fell back to issue some orders to the man in charge of the baggage cart, and in a little while his principal retainer, James White, came forward to lead the way to Kilkenny.

He was impossible. How could I ever understand him? It occurred to me that it would be a terrible thing to be in love with a man like Piers.

I could not get him out of my mind.

Dear God, could such a fate be happening to me?

CHAPTER 5

Kilkenny Castle proved to be much like Maynooth in size and structure. There the resemblance ended. Where Maynooth was set on a sunny plain, surrounded by crystal lakes, Kilkenny brooded over craggy, windswept and, it seemed to me, perpetually misty highlands. Maynooth, managed by Mother's caring hand, was bright with tapestries and fire and candlelight. The floors were often swept, the rushes changed often. Kilkenny was damp and cold, lit only by a few torches stuck in brackets in the dank, dripping walls. The rushes looked as though they'd been there since the time of Saint Patrick, the beds had no hangings nor was there glass in any of the narrow windows, so that cold and rain dashed in at will and the castle was under the indifferent chatelaineship of a dull-witted, slatternly woman from the village.

Piers was nearly as appalled as I when we'd settled down to live in the great pile of stone. Previously, being much in England or Waterford on business, he'd seldom stayed at Kilkenny. Its very state of decay and neglect, however, served to help me adjust to life away from home and family. I had to be a Butler's wife, I thought grimly; I didn't have to live in Butler squalor.

The very day of my arrival, I began instituting changes that made the old woman, Maude Goodfellow, take to her heels for her daughter-in-law's cottage, muttering through toothless gums that it was Godless to be so concerned about a few fleas in one's bedding. I attacked the filthy rushes on the floors, often needing a spade to lift them, dank and abominable from the stone floors, hauled them into a corner of the stableyard to be added to the compost heap, dragged out every stinking straw-filled bedtick in the place to be burned, which required that we sleep on the bedboards until new mattresses and bedding could be brought from Flanders, and sent to the chandlers in Waterford for a large supply of candles. I ordered fires laid and oiled paper to be put across the windows until we could have glass installed.

As Piers watched with ill-concealed pleasure the changes I made at Kilkenny, he told me to send to the village for some lasses to help me. Even I, Margaret Fitzgerald, he said mockingly, could not scrub a castle single-handed.

It was soon fit for human habitation, anyhow. And, with the fleas and grubs and unhousebroken hounds turned out, I'd have time to put my needle to work making bed hangings. Even the walls were less damp, and I began working a tapestry I'd drawn depicting Queen Deirdre, whose black sorrows overwhelmed her and who, like I, had been given in marriage where her heart lay not.

I had seen a huge rock near a small burn in a stony glen that I thought would be a good model for that rock Deirdre's captor's chariot had struck, throwing her out to her death, and, when a soft day in early spring found me free of the most pressing duties, I took a sketch pad and went to draw it for the tapestry.

I had settled down and managed a passable sketch when Piers came down the bank opposite, as I had done, leaped the burn and stood looking down at me. He smiled and nodded approvingly at the sketch in my lap.

I had noticed he often chanced to be near when I walked or rode out, and I believed he enjoyed my company. Indeed, though we were often prickly and defensive with each other, nearly any mention of politics finding us at odds, we seemed to be growing closer too, finding common interests as well as the widely disparate viewpoints our family backgrounds had engendered. I did not go out of my way to be with him, but it was only from pride that I did not now. Privately, I had to admit that I was coming to care very deeply about him. Oddly, though his temperament was nothing like my fiery father's, his character was very like. He cared about the people in his charge and saw to their health and well-being, nor were his rents exorbitant. He dealt with wrongdoings at the manor court with justice, neither too hard nor too easy a penalty for those who erred, so that, on the whole, Kilkenny was a peaceful, contented demesne. Unlike Father, he never wore Irish dress and encouraged me not to by gifting me lavishly with fine fabrics from Waterford to be sewed into English gowns. In short, it was becoming harder and harder for me to stay aloof from him. Indeed, he seemed less stubborn than I at trying to bridge the differences between us.

Now he dropped an apple into my lap and sat down beside me, polishing a second one for himself on his sleeve.

"That is very good, Margaret. I've seen for myself that you're efficient and cleanly and much skilled at chatelaineship, but I didn't suspect you were also an artist."

"Thank you," I said, laying the sketch on a slanted rock so he could inspect it and picking up the apple, "for the compliment and the apple." I smiled at him and took a bite, thinking for the thousandth time it was a pity he was a Butler. He was so much like the gallant knight I'd dreamed of all my life, save only in his appearance and his contempt for all things romantic or sentimental. Perhaps, just perhaps, I ought to modify my standards a little.

A skylark flew from a greening treetop, voicing liquid joy, and the cascading water soothed and lulled. I was suddenly aware of the great beauty and isolation of the little glen and that Piers was staring at me with an expression I couldn't read in his eyes. My own pulse quickened and I remembered the two times he'd embraced me and a deep, sweet longing filled me. But I could never let him see that. I'd told him I'd never submit to him. And Margaret Fitzgerald was not the lass to humble herself. Yet his hair was thick and glossy and tumbled over his forehead so enticingly I longed to entangle my fingers in it, feel its texture. His eyes were gentle for all his cynical speech sometimes, and his arms were powerful and slender with a look of strength leashed until needed; his smile was lovely entirely, and all at once, for a precious moment, he was not a Butler but my beloved Piers. I was delighted with him, friend and companion, and I longed to have him as husband . . . and lover too. I turned my eyes toward my sketch so he'd not see the longing in them.

"I am deeply grateful to you, Margaret, for all you've done to Kilkenny. It *is* mine to all intents and purposes, since Uncle Thomas will never willingly live here and I am his heir. I had, of course, hoped to make it more comfortable once I was living here permanently, but I never dreamed the old pile of stone could be so lovely. It's all due to you."

"I only cleaned it."

He laughed silently. "Aye. Do you know what the servants call you? 'The Lady of the Suds.'"

I laughed too. "No doubt they wish me on the moon. They seem to have had an easy life before I came and stirred things up."

"Nay, on the contrary. I think they like you and are very proud of Kilkenny's chatelaine. After all, until you came it was only a crumbling old castle. You have made it a home."

"By cleaning out the sour rushes?" I said smiling.

"It's more than that. You've given it grace . . . comfort . . . oh, I can't explain it." He seemed to search for words. "Perhaps it is that I have never truly had a home of my own before. My parents both died when I was so young, and Uncle Thomas, though he was kind to me, had been in exile here at Kilkenny—unhappily so, too. It never seemed more than a shelter before. My aunt had died and her two daughters, my cousins, were married to Englishmen. Uncle Thomas had married again before Edward IV came to the throne and had a poor wight of a daughter whose mind was blank. I think she's likely in convent by now; there seemed no other recourse for her than to be cared for by the nuns. At any rate, his second wife would not leave

England when my uncle was forced into exile, and so Kilkenny was a sad place with no woman's gentle touch."

"Ah, I'm sorry for that, Piers," I said softly, "for you have missed much, then. Always, for me as I grew up, there was grace and beauty and laughter. Mother kept Maynooth happy . . . almost a heaven on earth, it was . . ." I trailed off, suddenly acutely homesick. But then, at least I had known the kindly stuff of home, and Piers never had. I was suddenly moved by pity for him and understood why he was so self-contained and unsentimental. No one had ever taught him to show the affection we exuberant Fitzgeralds took for granted.

"It will be beautiful for you when I have had time to work some hangings," I said gently, indicating the sketch. "I will do what I can to make it a real home."

He smiled into my eyes and we shared a fine moment entirely. Then, suddenly, he threw the apple over his shoulder exultantly and reached for me. Our movement toward each other was as smooth as if we'd been practicing daily, our lips meeting as truly as Ireland is beautiful. There, on that soft spring day, with only the sound of the new growing and the burn chuckling at the inevitable, I finally, truly, became Piers's wife. It was all I'd hoped it would be in the days of my girlhood and more than I could have ever known.

Yet, afterward, he spoiled it by lifting himself on his elbow and flashing me a smile full of mockery.

"I told you you'd like it," he said exultantly, almost gloatingly.

I stifled a desire to hit him. Why couldn't he say something appropriately tender? But then, remembering his telling of his bleak childhood, I sighed in resignation.

"You were quite right," I said, forcing a smile. It was, after all, foolish to expect endearments from Piers, and the sooner I learned it the better.

"Then, there will be no more foolishness about refusing me your bed?"

"I suppose it is a stupid thing to do," I agreed.

"You liked it too much to deny me now," he said smugly.

I pushed him away and clambered to my feet.

"You are the most arrogant, self-satisfied . . ."

But he grabbed me around the knees and toppled me over, quickly enfolding me again. His laughter was only cut off when he brought his lips down over my mouth again.

And that was how it was to be with us.

Piers had won again.

Yet, that is not to say that I was unhappy with him. Indeed, as long as I didn't let my romantic heart run away with me, I was deeply content as chatelaine of Kilkenny and Piers Butler's wife. I knew that he was well-content too. He worked hard administering his uncle's affairs and turned to me increasingly to discuss any problems on the estates. There was never any question that we liked and respected each other. We relied on each other entirely, each doing his share of the duties connected with Kilkenny, and often more, so that the old castle prospered and grew lovely. We spent our days in hard work and many a night in warm embraces. That is not to say, however, that overnight we became as one. Indeed, often we struck sparks from each other, as Piers called it, blaming it all on my "Fitzgerald pride," as I blamed his "Butler arrogance."

Yet, he respected my family greatly, especially Father. Paradoxically, he seemed to have trouble sometimes laying aside our ancient animosity. He didn't like to be compared unfavorably to my father, and, though I ought to be ashamed to tell it, I soon learned this was the only weak chink in his armor of arrogance and was not above using it when he angered me. Mother had only to write that Father had established a school at Maynooth, and Piers would establish a bigger one at Kilkenny village.

He seldom left Kilkenny except on the most urgent of business for his uncle, for his cousin continued to roam

Ireland, growing even bolder in pillage and rape and murder. Piers wrote to his Uncle Thomas, who was chamberlain to Queen Elizabeth and a member of the king's council, protesting furiously and, for the most part, impotently. Uncle Thomas would reply that the king used Sir James and the Garths, father and son, to teach "Our Irish Rebel, Kildare," a lesson. So Piers never left Kilkenny unless he was certain his cousin was too far away to raid it in his absence. And, unfortunately, he was seldom far off enough for Piers to be willing to take me to Maynooth for a visit. I wasn't quite certain whether he was truly alarmed for my safety should we chance to engage his cousin, or whether he just was too jealous of my father to want to visit my home. Which caused me a certain amount of resentment. So, though we were moving toward a trusting relationship, it was not entirely idyllic and disagreements were frequent, with Piers turning stony-silent and uncommunicative and I furious entirely. On the whole, though, I was content.

Except that I longed to conceive and didn't.

Isolated as we were in our little world of Kilkenny, though, we were well-informed of how matters stood in England and the rest of Ireland by letters from Piers's Uncle Thomas and from Mother. We had not left home nor had the family there at Maynooth, though, because of the unsettled condition of the country. Black James had created total anarchy and folk sheltered behind barred doors, except for the wild Irish chieftains who raided and pillaged, scarcely deterred now that Father had been removed as deputy and replaced by his wily, old enemy, the Archbishop of Dublin, Walter Fitzsimmonds. So incensed had Father been by that perfidious move on the king's part that he'd taken to roaming and killing a bit himself. Which made Piers remark that two wrongs didn't make a right, leading to my defending Father's actions and blaming it all on the Butlers.

Just before Christmas of the following year, 1492, Thomas Garth killed Eleanor's betrothed, Calvagh O'Con-

nor Faly in a raid that was treacherous entirely. Mother
wrote that Eleanor was quite destroyed by grief and that,
when Father got the news, he'd roared out of Maynooth at
the head of his own troops and annihilated Garth's squad
of soldiers, killing the younger Garth and imprisoning Sir
Thomas, the father. Which had gotten him into even more
trouble with the king and not done poor Eleanor any good
except giving her the satisfaction of revenge for her beloved's death. Then, in January of 1493, taking revenge in
his turn, Sir James Butler had led another skirmish against
Conn More O'Neill, Father's favorite brother-in-law, killing the big man and leaving his small son as the head of
O'Neill. They'd betrothed him and Alice, Mother said,
which was Father's way of extending his protection to our
cousin, young Conn, and warning Black James that any
further action against the tanist of O'Neill would be taken
as a personal assault on Father.

Then did the king demand Father send young Gerry to
England as hostage so Father could no longer "commit
depredations against the king's subjects." Now, our parents had always intended sending Gerry to England to be
educated at the English court, as was our custom among
the Anglo-Irish lords, but they were not about to surrender
him as hostage to Henry of England. So Father himself
was off to England, attempting in vain to refute the lying
charges of Black James and his holy toady, the archbishop.

But at last, in the summer of 1493, even the King of
England seemed to get his craw full of Black James and
Walter Fitzsimmonds, for he removed the fat prelate as
deputy to the viceroy. Drunk with the power Father's dis-
favor in England had given them, the odious duet had
called a perfidious Parliament accusing Father of outra-
geous crimes, formally attainting Baron Portlester, Grandfather FitzEustace, and ordering Piers's Uncle Thomas to
come back to Ireland and live on his lands, which they
well knew he could not, being in vital service to the king,
or forfeit them to Sir James along with the honor of Ormonde! So the king removed him as deputy and sent the

neutral Sir Robert Preston to act in the post for the time being.

Then off went Black James and the archbishop to pick holes in Father's coat at the king's court. And off went Father in exasperated pursuit to try to defend himself. Perkin Warbeck had been gathering adherents on the Continent, and, although Father had had no further dealings with him, Black James, neatly playing on the king's almost abnormal fear of pretenders, had convinced him that Warbeck had been again in Ireland, supported by Father, Uncle Maurice of Desmond, as we called Father's cousin, and most of the wild Irish who loved and respected Father.

In September of 1494, tired of the constant running back and forth across the channel with tales on the part of the two parties, the king had sent both Father and Black James back to Ireland to "try and behave themselves" in the company of one Sir Edward Poynings, who was to take over the deputyship and lead the army of some six or seven hundred he'd brought along. It seemed, though, that he was little better than Black James and far from unbiased, for Black James's army of a thousand promptly joined forces with the English army against Father.

Uncle Thomas wrote from England that Poynings was as cruel and dissolute a man as was known in England, having browbeaten (and, 'twas rumored, beaten in actuality) his little wife and a virtual harem of mistresses who traveled with him everywhere. He had a large number of children from these mistresses and had been suspected of sexually mistreating them too, boys and girls. We were appalled at this news. How could the king loose a monster like that on Ireland? Couldn't he understand the resentment, the potential trouble he was causing in Ireland, by this course of humiliating and degrading us? Even Piers had to admit that my father would never be other than loyal to the English crown were there no Yorkists to follow, and he'd long since had to admit that there were not. And Father's rule was just and righteous. He ruled the Irish not because of his Englishness but because of his Irishness.

In any case, the outcome of Sir Edward Poynings' occupation of Ireland meant vicissitudes and trouble for everyone except Black James. He convinced Poynings that Father and his friend Hugh Roe O'Donnell, head of the family that ruled all the north of Ireland, were in cahoots with James of Scotland and Perkin Warbeck against the king, and the only thing to be done was to lead the army against Hugh Roe. Father, protesting furiously, had no choice but to go along on the campaign, hoping to prove the falsity of the charges.

Thus matters stood on December 1, 1494, when, just at first dark, Grandfather FitzEustace arrived attended by only his "squire," young Michael, the page who'd lowered the drawbridge at Maynooth against us at Alice's command nearly three years before, now grown tall and broad with a thousand freckles still and an engaging grin.

Grandfather looked thin, but fit and wiry as ever. His eyes, bluer than I remembered, lit up with unabashed joy when they fell on me. He clambered down agilely from his aged horse, throwing the reins toward Michael.

"Grandfather. Ah, Grandfather, my darling man," I screamed happily, throwing myself at him. Then, realizing his appearance at Kilkenny was not the ordinary thing with the state the country was in, I held him at arm's length and stared worriedly into his face.

"Grandfather, what are you doing here? And so ill-attended?" I said anxiously. "Is all well at Maynooth? Or Father . . . no one's dead, surely . . ."

"No, lass. Those at Maynooth are . . . much as you left them. But that Goddamned Black James Butler—begging your pardon, Piers," he added as my husband came out to stand behind and above me on the stairs—"has convinced Poynings that your father was plotting to kill him, the king's own appointed deputy, once they reached the O'Donnell territory."

"And Poynings believed him?" Piers said stridently.

"Aye. At least he pretended to, wanting, I've no doubt, an excuse to arrest your father-in-law. Gerald has taken to the heather somewhere in the O'Hanlon country."

"Will that black bastard never have done with plaguing the Geraldines?" I cried.

Piers moved suddenly down the stairs, whistling for one of our castle people to take the horses and bring in the saddlebags.

"Come, Grandfather FitzEustace," he said kindly, "come into my house and God give you welcome. You are wet through. When we've fed and warmed you both, you can tell us all that's happened."

Piers was always sensible, I thought with the now-familiar mingling of exasperation and longing, as I followed them into the great hall.

Later, as Michael and Grandfather finished eating, Piers poured them good measures of cider, mulling it with the hot poker.

"Do you think, sir," Piers said, "that my word that your son-in-law is incapable of such plotting would carry any weight with this Poynings?"

"'Tis why I've come to fetch you to Maynooth," Grandfather said warmly. "I'd not the slightest doubt you'd want to help. Ah, a sorry, black time for Ireland it is, man."

"If you're going, so am I," I said. "How I've missed them all."

Piers stared at me in the enigmatic way I'd come to know. Never could I read the thoughts behind his dark eyes. Was he about to forbid me venturing out into the unsettled country? I lifted my chin as if to warn him he'd better not try, and he smiled ironically and put down his cup.

"Aye, wife, I'll take a goodly guard."

"How are they, Grandfather?" I said, turning to him to hide my relief that defiance hadn't been necessary, for Piers was no more capable of being ruled by a woman than my own father was.

Grandfather frowned and shook his head. "There's not the slightest use of me pretending all is well, Magheen," he said, "for it isn't. Eleanor has grieved herself to a shadow for her dead Calvagh, and your mother's near distraught over this latest indignity the king's forced on us. Having Poynings and the army billeted at Maynooth early in the fall was bad enough, but this new accusation against Gerald and his turning fugitive has been almost too much for her."

"Are you up to starting back at first light?" Piers said.

"Aye, man, I hoped you'd say that," Grandfather said, eyes flashing satisfaction. "I've not been out of the saddle since I left the army, but I couldn't rest more than was necessary until I've done all I can for Gerald."

"*You* were with Gerait More, Grandfather FitzEustace?" Piers said with admiration.

"Aye. He had twelve of his best besides me with him when he took to the heather, and I'd have gone too, only there was none other to take word to my daughter. They little thought, the cursed Lancastrians, that I was aught but a potty old man. They'll never think I would come to you for help." His eyes filled with soft tears that he dashed away with his long, artist's hands. "I'd go to the ends of the earth to get help for Gerait More," he said grimly.

We started back to Maynooth, well guarded by Piers's strongest men-at-arms at cockcrow in the morning, December 2, and reached there on Saint Nicholas Eve, December 5. I realized with a start it had been exactly three years since Perkin Warbeck's visit to Maynooth. I wished bitterly that we'd never heard of him. I had thought him comely and dreamed of riding at his side to conquer England. Had all my girlish dreams come true and he'd been the true heir of England with a guarantee of winning the throne of England, I'd not have abandoned my Piers to marry him, though, like as not, Piers being a good Lancastrian, we'd have had to flee into exile.

But I would die rather than admit that to Piers.

Maynooth looked much as it had when I'd left it, a high-hearted girl of eighteen. But it didn't *sound* the same. The raucous and contented roar that usually filled hall and court was gone entirely. The great castle brooded in sullen silence as if mourning its absent master. Walter, left behind by Father to look after Mother and the children, bullied the castle lads and lasses as of old, but the heart seemed gone from Maynooth, and, indeed, it was woefully understaffed. Most of the best men-at-arms had gone with Father, and many of the others were off defending their own smaller demesnes. For the first time in my remembrance, no Yule log had been brought in on Saint Nicholas Eve, no preparations or chatter about issuing forth into the woods to gather the holly and ivy had been undertaken.

My little brother and sisters were subdued and jumpy. Gerry, now eight, was a credit to Maynooth with his quiet intelligence and beguiling air of being the man in charge with my father gone. Eustacia was as beautiful at nearly three as she'd promised to be as an infant. She hung back, not knowing me and shy, clinging to Beth's skirts. Beth was as gentle and pious as ever. Her beads were never far from her hands even in the old days; now, maturing and obviously aware of the trouble that brooded over Maynooth, she fingered them constantly. Alice had changed most of all. She had been a homely child with her newly sprouted two front teeth preponderous as a hare's when I'd left home; the three years had been beneficial entirely to her. She had grown tall, up to my shoulder already, and her resemblance to Father, still marked, had softened and feminized so that she promised to be a great beauty someday. She was neither so noisy nor mischievous as she'd been then, either. Eleanor, my dear Nelly, was more silent and lovely than she'd ever been, her slender form honed to a thinness that made her beautiful blue eyes seem sunken and shadowed, although, when I gazed into them, I could see it was the loss of her Calvagh that truly caused the dark shadows.

I was troubled by the change in all my family, but it

wasn't until I ran up to Mother's chamber and saw what
had become of her that I was filled with a shaking, glorious rage at Black James.

She lay on the great bed where all of us had been conceived and born. Her tiring-woman held her in her arms
while she retched feebly into a basin. So thin was she that
she scarcely made a mound under the coverlet she'd
worked herself.

"Mother, dearest love, you're ill," I cried, running to the
bedside to embrace her. She turned huge gray eyes upon
me, and her smile, welcoming and glad to see me, was
quickly gone in the greater pain of my father's absence.

"I'm only pregnant, Magheen," she hastened to reassure
me. "The sickness that happens sometimes in the early
months. If your father were here, I'd be well enough."

I drew her into my arms and kissed her forehead. It was
clammy, and the skin was stretched paper-thin across the
bones. It was as white as paper too, not glowing with
pearly tones as it had always been. Her hair lay scattered
across the pillow the color of a pumpkin seen through a
ruby, but with patches of silver shaped like a kitten's ears
at each temple. She was thin, too thin to be with child, her
fingers reaching to capture mine like the bones of a starve-
ling bird.

"Pregnant, Mother?" I said, hiding my concern with an
effort.

"No one knows, Magheen, except Agnes here. Never
could I hide that circumstance from her. Even your sister
Nell hasn't learned." Her eyes filled with tears. "I didn't
know when your father went with Poynings, though,
heaven knows, I'd not have told him when he had no
choice but to go anyhow. Ah, Magheen, thank Blessed
Mary you've come. They've put a price on his head, darling. Every cutthroat in Ireland will be watching for him
. . ." Her voice broke and she turned her head to and fro
on the pillow as if to escape intolerable pain.

"Mother, none among the Irish will harm him," I said
sternly, though I was greatly worried about him too.

"Think you any hand would be raised against Gerait More? Why, there's not a one in Ireland except some of the Butlers and O'Briens who'd not shelter and hide him. Nor does Poynings know the hills and heather well enough to pursue him. Put your heart at ease, Mother. You'll harm the babe you carry if you continue like this, and that would be a grief to Father entirely."

She struggled to gain control of herself at that. "You are right, child. Magheen, Magheen, my darling, it's so good to have you home, regardless of the reason. But it's you, not an aging woman like myself, who ought to be with child."

"That is as God wills, Mother," I said, trying to speak nonchalantly, for her problems were so great I didn't want to burden her with my sorrow at the fact I had not as yet conceived. "You must take care of yourself," I scolded, "for you aren't as young as you were when us older children were born. Eustacia was a surprise, and that was three years ago. You must really try to stay serene and put your heart at rest."

She made a brave attempt to smile. "I . . . I . . . had planned to tell your father on Christmas Eve . . . as a precious gift to him," she said, her voice breaking.

"You may yet, indeed. Don't give up hope, Mother. Poynings may abandon the chase as useless and go back to England."

She considered and seemed to find comfort in such a possibility.

"He'll say, 'By Saint Bride, Lady, that's the best news I've had since Eustacia was born,'" she said in a creditable imitation of Father's voice. We laughed together.

Agnes smiled, showing several gaps where teeth had been lost.

"Magheen, you darling girl, my prayers are answered that you've found means to make my lady leave off weeping," she said.

"We have missed you so much, Magheen," Mother said. "Oh, if only Black James would cease stirring the king up against us. If only Ireland were at peace so we could visit back and forth . . ."

"At least he's removed his puppet, the archbishop, from the deputyship, Mother. Perhaps he is finally learning what a rogue and troublemaker the man is. Perhaps he'll go a bit too far and land himself in the Tower. Then the king will see that Father's been ruling in the king's best interest all along."

"It had better be soon, darling, for we're at the mercy of the army now. There are no more than six men at Maynooth; the others went with your father, and when he was accused, only twelve of them got away with him. The rest are under guard in the English camp."

"Do you think they'd dare attack Maynooth?"

"Aye. I've been afraid of it."

"Piers has brought a troop of five," I said.

"Small defense if they bring the army against us."

"Ah, Mother, even the Clanricarde Burkes have too much honor to attack Maynooth and Father in the heather," I said in disgust. "This Poynings must be an animal."

"A fit companion for that Black James, Lady Magheen," Agnes said indignantly, "which tells you all you need to know of his character."

"We must hope for the best. Piers has come along. When Poynings returns to Dublin, he means to talk to him, explain that Father wouldn't behave treacherously to save his soul."

"Bless him. Have you come, then, to love him, Magheen?"

I hesitated for a long moment. How could I tell her that I had come to love him with all my heart but that he only made the best of marriage to a Fitzgerald? Or so it seemed to me. "Aye, Mother," I said at last. "I love him. Now go to sleep."

Piers was pacing back and forth nervously in the room we were to share.

"No one seems to know where Poynings is, Margaret," he said when I came in.

"He probably hardly knows where he is himself," I said grimly. "He'll have a time of it, keeping order when the Irish hear Father's taken to the heather."

"God, Margaret, your father's a greater fool than even I imagined, and heaven knows I've been vastly aware of his foolishness this long while."

It was an old argument, but I rose to it as eagerly as ever.

"How can you blame him for foolishness this time? *He's* not to blame for your cousin's lies and slanders."

"He should never have run. Couldn't he see that his taking to his heels was almost an admission of guilt? Why didn't he stand and demand a fair trial on the charges?"

"You think he'd have gotten a fair trial in a Lancastrian court?" I asked scornfully.

"Margaret, when are you going to stop that partisan prate? Your father's been treated most justly. Believe me, your Yorkist kings of such blessed memory would have had his head on a pike over London Bridge long ago had he dealt with them the way he has with King Henry. Now I thought he'd settled down and developed a bit of common sense. But he hasn't a sensible bone in his whole body."

"Sensible, sensible, sensible," I snapped. "Is that the only virtue you know? How dare you sit in judgment of my father! He's not as sensible as you, but if you live to be a thousand you'll not have all the love he has in his heart. Yes, *love*. But that virtue is obviously obnoxious to you. He's loving and trusting and doesn't know how to deal with the intrigues of the Tudor *sensibly*. So the likes of your black-hearted cousin can get him into difficulties he has no way of getting out of."

"Oh, quit canonizing Gerait More," he shouted back. "I'm sick of hearing how good and trusting and simple he is. He's about as 'simple' as a Temple Bar lawyer. It's all a carefully cultivated facade, a ploy to get his own way. Yet, he's stupid too, and has involved his whole family. Your mother . . ."

"You leave my mother out of this," I cried, realizing he was partially right. "She's pregnant and ill and I'm worried about her."

That sobered him and distracted him from his anger.

"Is she, then, Margaret?" Seeing by my face that she was, he dropped down to sit on the edge of the coffer under a window. He seemed lost in thought, and when he spoke at last his anger seemed all gone.

"I hope your mother doesn't understand how grave matters are," he said.

Despite our differences, however, we soon had need to lay them aside in the interests of Maynooth and the family. The day after our arrival, Poynings laid siege to the castle.

"He can't believe Gerald is here," Grandfather cried when we awoke to find the plain around Maynooth rapidly growing smaller as the English army, surrounding us from far out, marched rapidly inward, causing all the villagers and farmers of our demesne lands to flee inward toward the castle.

By midmorning, the outer ward of the castle was filled with the refugees, women and children for the most part, since many of the men were with Father or off in the heather, fighting the wild Irish. They'd not had time to bring with them more than a handful of dried peas. The harvest had not been good nor had the men been home for the butchering at Michaelmas, so Maynooth was in no condition to feed so many extra mouths. Yet we hadn't enough men to fight. There was nothing for it but to ration out the little we had and hope we could last until someone came to help.

Piers went up to the battlements to try to reason with Poynings when he'd drawn close enough to hear.

"There is no use besieging Maynooth, Sir Edward," he

shouted. "Gerait More is not here. We have no more idea than you where he is."

But his declaration was met with derisive laughter. "Take care, Piers Butler, that you don't fall into treason from association," Poynings called back, then stalked away out of earshot, as though he disdained to so much as exchange words with Maynooth.

"Perhaps we ought to let him in," Piers said, puzzled. "If he sees Gerait's gone, he'll stop wasting time on a worthless siege that can only distress the Lady Allison . . ."

But Grandfather protested vehemently.

"God, lad, 'tis easy to see you've seldom served in an army," he cried. "They'd steal everything, including the collar off the Kildare ape's crest. Besides, that would be the least of it . . . while I doubt they'd touch the Fitzgerald women, the village girls would be fair game for them."

"Grandfather FitzEustace, I may not have served in the army but I know King Henry forbade any of that sort of thing upon pain of death at Bosworth and Stoke. And there was no looting or rape. This is his army too."

"But under Poynings. And this is Ireland. He doesn't consider us true Englishmen to be protected," Grandfather said with growing agitation. "No, no, I must override you, Piers. We can't let them gain access to Maynooth. It will stand forever. Perhaps Gerald will hear of our plight. Or James, his brother. He's been riding at the head of a large troop since Poynings descended on us so vengefully."

Piers saw that it was useless to argue with Grandfather and went away to take inventory of what food we had on hand.

It proved woefully inadequate.

Christmas was the worst, with the little ones talking of the boar's head and comfits we'd had in years past. Piers had contrived to save one small keg of ale and, after Christmas Mass in the small family chapel, everyone had a meager thimbleful along with the half-cup of oatmeal we were reduced to twice a day. I silently cursed our tormentors, Christmas Day though it was, for reducing us to such straits. If Father had been here these past weeks, even with the poor harvest, there'd have been meat curing in the sheds from the Michaelmas slaughter, and the grain bins would have been full, though it might have meant he'd had to send clear to Spain for a shipload. I realized, woefully, how vulnerable my family was with only gallant old Grandfather to see to their well-being. Mother, always so steady and dependable, was dreadfully ill, not only with her pregnancy but with fear for Father. I thought of Piers's comment that he hoped she didn't truly understand how grave matters were, but I knew in her heart she did. Her only comfort was that Father was safe in the heather. They'd never find him as long as he stayed out. And the longer Maynooth could withstand the siege, the greater his chance to gather forces and rescue us.

Our supplies dwindled further. Fortunately, there was plenty of somewhat brackish water from a well within the walls, but our people began to sicken.

Nell and Piers and I had been doling out the daily ration, each person coming forward in the great hall with a wooden bowl to receive his. The children got as much as the adults, which was meager enough, but, even so, there was one family, the tanner's wife and children, who'd always been thin as pikes but with appetites big enough for blacksmiths, and their spindliness was terrible to behold.

As we ladled out the allotments one morning, Piers motioned me to hand the dipper over to Nell and follow him. When we were clear of the others, he leaned over and spoke softly near my ear.

"Where is your grandfather, Margaret?"

"He took his bowl and went off with it," I said, looking around the hall. "Here somewhere, I suppose."

"He's not stayed here with the others to eat these three days now," he said worriedly. "And you know how sociable he is. I think he's disobeyed the rule that everyone's to eat his own allotment. I watched his direction. Come."

I followed him and we reached the passage to the

kitchen just in time to see him disappear through it. There were sculleries beyond where the tanner's family had been staying, they having children small enough to suffer from the cold of the stables.

We crossed the kitchen and reached the far door just in time to see Grandfather lurch to his knees, proffering his bowl to the poor meager mother, who took it silently and began spooning it to each of the listless children in turn.

"Where is the baby, Katherine?" Grandfather said.

"Ah, milord, she died in the night," was the reply in a voice so expressionless it emphasized our sorry plight the more. It was as though the poor woman had accepted the inevitable, that none of us could ever get out of it alive.

But Grandfather's old face crumpled like a child's who's been whipped unfairly. Always he had worried about the little ones, his blood and those he chanced to encounter. His emaciated frame shook with his weeping and he pitched forward, fainting from his own deprivation.

Piers and I managed to get him laid out in a more comfortable position while one of the children went for Nell and Alice to help us get him up to bed, for, in truth, none of us was overly strong by now.

And when we'd gotten him into his bed and a bit of thin porridge into him, he opened his eyes and stared at Piers.

"Go, Piers, go lower the bridge," he said.

We all assembled in the great hall, except for Mother and the children and Grandfather. The women wept silently, holding their weakened children in their arms, their faces grim and scared. Piers came to stand beside me and put his arm around my shoulders and I turned my face to his, feeling his grief and barely suppressed rage, and, despite the horror of the siege, it was good to feel the comradeship between us two. I thought that, without him, I'd never have had the courage to face the English troops.

They had taken the time to come ceremonially, giving him time to reach my side after ordering the bridge lowered.

Poynings and Black James came first, their standard
bearers beside them. Black James was as resplendent in his
dark armor as if he'd been in a tournament parade, and
Poynings seemed like a surfeited leech to me. He was huge
and gross, with small eyes glinting with cruelty and a
mouth that worked perpetually, almost as if he were taking a lascivious enjoyment from our condition.

"Where is the countess and the heir of Kildare?" Poynings barked. "Bring them here at once."

We heard a small noise from the main stair, and in a
moment Grandfather came lurching into view, stumbling
across the great hall to stand before Poynings.

"My daughter, Lady Allison, is very ill and her son is
only eight years old," he said with dignity. "We have surrendered Maynooth to you; I pray you, be merciful."

Poynings laughed unpleasantly and nodded to the soldiers, who swarmed throughout the hall.

"Find them," he snapped.

They ran toward the various tower stairs, knocking
Grandfather over. Piers and I ran to help him but were
both jerked back and quickly immobilized by several men.
Grandfather, too, was pulled erect, though so weak was he
that his captor seemed to be supporting him rather than
imprisoning him.

In a short while, of course, they were dragging Mother
and Gerry across the hall, Eustacia and Beth screaming
with terror and stumbling along behind.

Mother's appearance was terrifying. Her eyes were like
bits of wet charcoal that had stained the hollows below
them. She had no more flesh than the poor tanner's family,
and the soldier who'd found her was nearly carrying her,
his arm around her waist, her thin arm across his shoulder.
I thought he looked pitying.

But there was no pity in Poynings' small eyes.

Mother faced him bravely. "If you have been besieging
us in hopes of capturing my husband, I fear you will be
disappointed," she said defiantly. "I honestly don't know

where he is. So, even should you put me to torture, it will do you no good."

"Surely, Lady Allison, you are not so simple that you believe we hoped to capture *Gerait More*," he drawled.

He strode the short distance to my little brother and grabbed the collar of his tunic, jerking him away from the soldier who held him, and tightly against his own fat belly.

"We have the cub now, the old bear will quickly come in."

We all lunged forward furiously—myself, Nell, Alice, Piers and Grandfather. All were far too securely held to escape except for my grandfather, who'd been in such a state of collapse the soldier holding him had little thought he'd be able to interfere.

The old man was half the size of Poynings in his frame and probably a third in weight, but he was screaming our war cry and striking out with fury entirely.

A simple push from Poynings would have been enough. But he whipped a dagger from his belt so swiftly that only the quick flash of silver betrayed it. Grandfather cried out in pain and slumped against a pillar. His left cheek gaped open from near the eye to the corner of his mouth and blood rushed to the stones, bathing his doublet and hands.

Piers's face was contorted with rage, and through a haze of fury and pain I realized there was a high keening in the hall, the women wailing in sorrow and impotence, and my own voice, to my great surprise, was part of it, and not of my own volition but of instinct entirely.

"Off to Westminster with you, milad," Poynings said merrily. Then he turned deliberately to Mother, holding Gerry close. "By the rood, Lady Allison, when you *are* in touch with your husband, you might tell him that it's entirely up to him whether this lad is placed in the maiden wing as a playmate for Prince Hal . . . or trained as a catamite for me."

With one horrible moan, Mother fainted mercifully away. The man-at-arms who held her, swung her easily up into his arms and carried her back up the tower stairs.

Then did I scream, *"Goddamned bloated Lancastrian pig"* and Gaelic obscenities I'd never voiced before. I could have torn his little piggy eyes out of his head myself if they'd only have released me.

Black James came to stand before me, laughing in triumph.

"Ah, Margaret, anger and hunger only heighten your beauty. Come, show me where you sleep . . ."

Piers was a wild man, lunging for his cousin's throat, but a vicious blow to the face felled him and he lay, unmoving, at my feet.

Poynings made an impatient gesture with the bloody knife he still held. "Not now, you damned fool. God knows, I'm not the man to deny you what pleasure you'd take in such a bony wench, but our business right now is to get this lad manacled aboard ship. And notices posted all over Ireland telling the father we have his son and will kill him unless he surrenders."

Black James nodded and threw me a mocking salute. "There'll be another time, Lady Margaret. 'Tis my destiny to have you."

For once in my life, I was too beaten and distraught to talk.

They left rapidly, pushing Gerry ahead of them. He strode out, his beautiful little head high, his thin wrists secured with a tightly lashed cord. Ah, he reminded me of Father, so gallant and brave, and I wept until I could no longer see anything but my own wavery tears and, through them, my husband inert and bleeding.

Then were we occupied, taking care of Grandfather and Piers. Nell sewed the terrible cut with a bit of white silk thread, and I washed Piers's cut mouth with cold water, finally awakening him. Except for the cut and a fierce headache, he seemed unharmed by the blow he'd taken and was soon ordering our people, now that the siege was lifted, to take what money we had and go range the Pale for food. There was likely to be little enough near Maynooth, with the army consuming everything that was edible.

But Piers was so angry he shook. I thought it was because of Poynings and Black James, and, as I handed him a cup of cider from a keg of such poor quality even the soldiers had disdained it, I smiled bitterly.

"Calm down, Piers, they've gone now. We've need of cool heads to figure what to do next . . ."

He tasted the cider and spat it to the rushes, then, with an oath, pushed the cup away and rounded on me. "Aye, well you might wonder what's to be done," he said with uncharacteristic vehemence. "God knows, *I* hardly know what to do. Your father's to blame for all of this."

"My father, is it? 'Twas *your* vile cousin who started it all. Had he not told the lies that got Father in trouble to start with, he'd not have run . . ."

"Ah, you can always find excuses for him. You're stiff-necked and blind and, yes, I fear, stupid, too, Margaret." he retorted.

"Because I see clearly that you're blaming my father for the evil your family started?" I cried furiously.

"Your entire family has a bad case of hero worship. You think that great blundering ape can do no wrong. Yet, look at the ruin he's brought on you, your mother and grandfather and poor little Gerry . . . and, God help me, I've no doubt now, the king will have a grievance against me as well for being here at Maynooth when it was in rebellion."

"Oh," I raged, "*now* we come to the crux of the matter, indeed. You're worried about your own sweet hide."

"Aye, I certainly am. And what's wrong with that? Why should I let the cursed Geraldines destroy me too?"

"And just what do you propose to do about it?"

He seemed to subside a little and stared at me, considering.

"I've a mind to go to England myself," he said, more to himself than to me. "If I make the most humble obeisance to His Highness I can, perhaps I can . . ."

"Oh, damn you, Piers Butler. Make humble obeisance,

indeed! After what he's done to my father? Well, then, go. Show your true colors. Abandon us in our need. You self-serving Butler. To think that I . . ."

His black eyes were intense. "That you *what*, Margaret?"

"That I . . . had to marry the likes of you," I snapped. Never would I say what I'd truly been thinking, *"that I have come to love you."*

He winced as his old mocking smile spread his cut lip, but he bowed with elaborate deference. "I will ride south, depart from Waterford or Cork, since I've no desire to confront Poynings again," he said, deliberately disregarding my verbal abuse. It was a way he had that only served to infuriate me the more.

"Go then, get out," I cried. "But, by the rood, leave the men you brought, for we've none other to defend us against your fine king's army."

"Nay, I'll take them along as far as Kilkenny, Margaret," he said reasonably, "for God knows what you'll use for food, else. But they'll be back with reinforcements in three days and with food to see you through the winter here."

"And you'll leave us to the army's mercy?" I said, still strident, though I had to swallow a lump of fear that was in my throat.

"You've nothing further to fear from the army, Margaret," he said grimly. "They've gotten what they want now."

"Your black cousin did not!" I snapped. "What if he comes back?"

His face paled and his jaw tightened, but, again in control of himself, he answered with his usual sensible deliberation.

"God help him if he attempts to tangle with you," he said dryly. "But you'd best stay within the walls, keep a double guard. And don't think of going back to Kilkenny until I return for you."

"*I'll* not return to Kilkenny," I cried, "never fear. I'm staying here with my own . . . where I belong . . . where

I'm needed . . . and *loved*. I'm a Fitzgerald, thank God, and I'll stay with my own."

"Suit yourself," he said with an indifferent shrug. He turned on his heel and stalked, none too steadily, up the stairs to gather his belongings.

The last I saw of him was from behind an outcropping of the battlements as he rode off, not looking back, toward the south. *I hated him. I hated him for abandoning me and for running to his miserable little clerk of a king to save his own hide.*

But, God help me, I loved him too. And I prayed to all our Irish saints and Saint Christopher as well that he'd brave the channel well. December seas could be tumultuous.

And within a few days of Gerry's capture and Piers's departure for England, on February 27, 1495, Father freely walked aboard the ship in Dublin Harbor where they held Gerry. He was promptly clapped into chains and taken off to England. There, we later learned, on March 5, he was lodged in the Tower of London and Gerry was remanded to the queen's custody.

CHAPTER 6

For many weeks we heard no news whatsoever from England. Winter storms, as though unleashing their fury that they had to give way to spring, kept shipping out of Saint George's Channel. But at last, in April, Piers's Uncle Thomas wrote to me at Maynooth, so I knew Piers had told him I was not at Kilkenny. At least, then, he'd cared enough to see that I had news of Father and Gerry, though he declined to write himself.

Gerry was under the protection of the queen herself, he wrote, and he saw him every day. The queen was quite taken with him and had given him the duties of one of her principal pages. As for Gerait More, he was being held in honorable confinement in the Tower of London, and, although he was allowed no visitors, he was quite safe, awaiting the king's pleasure, for the moment.

The wording was very careful; Sir Thomas would, of course, take heed to say nothing the king could misconstrue should his letter be read, but I felt he wanted me to know Poynings could not harm Gerry in the perverted way he'd threatened. The last phrase concerning Father, that he was safe *for the moment*, struck me as more than a little ominous, and I deliberately deleted it when I read his letter to Mother.

He did not, however, mention Piers.

Perhaps Piers had ordered him not to. Perhaps he had so far attempted to disengage himself from the fallen fortunes of Kildare that he was asking the king permission to apply for a divorce. We had no children; he could claim I'd denied him conjugal rights or something. Then he would be free to marry a staunch Lancastrian and regain

King Henry's favor. But how could he so far forget the companionship, the passionate nights, the hard work, and even the suffering of the siege we'd shared? I tortured myself with my imaginings and remembered guiltily that it was I who'd told him not to return.

Poynings had returned to Ireland after delivering Father and Gerry to the king, and, though he was a tyrant, his presence so close to Maynooth did tend to protect us from Black James, who, unaccountably, seemed suddenly to have fallen from the king's favor. Men said that Poynings kept the uneasy peace by paying enormous amounts of black rent to the wild Irish. I thought contemptuously that Father could have told him the folly of that. Sooner or later the money would be gone, and they'd descend again, bolder than ever.

Piers had sent more men and food and even a fresh goat back to Maynooth, as he'd promised, so at least we had food and men to defend us should Black James decide to brave the king's army.

But despite adequate food and the knowledge that Father and Gerry were alive, Maynooth's people were all badly demoralized.

Nell did her share of the work and more, but I knew she grieved for Calvagh far more than she ever mentioned. The three little girls, unnaturally subdued by all that had happened, followed Grandfather around as if to cling to something unchanged. Yet, even he, staunch old soldier that he was, had suffered greatly from the long siege. Always slender, he seemed almost emaciated now, nor did he gather flesh when the time of starving was over. His wounded cheek healed slowly and left a livid scar. He tried, in spite of all we did to dissuade him, to carry the work load of a man half his age and often dragged himself off to his bed before dark, too ill and weary to eat the evening meal.

As for Mother, she was so frail I feared she'd not live to deliver her babe. She believed it would be born near the end of June and tried valiantly to eat the food we urged on her, but she, like Grandfather, always thin, usually ended by retching most of what she'd patiently forced down. At last, too weak to leave her bed and existing on the goat's milk and soft bread which alone lay easy on her stomach, she had to give up even the needlework she loved. Then, bereft of work to keep her mind from her worries, she stared at the ceiling and wept.

There were times when I longed to do likewise. But I was the only one they all had to turn to. Someone had to stay in control, give orders to the frightened and demoralized castle people, see to the care of the children and our meager stock, and oversee the spring planting. Mercifully, spring *had* come early and gently munificent. There would be no hunger at Maynooth next winter. But with the chatelaine sick and the master gone off in disgrace, charged with treason and attempted murder, there was no joy and much apprehension among us.

And, watching the ruin my family had become, Nell, always so spirited and proud, bent with grief and work, Gerry and Father gone, Mother shattered entirely, I came to hate all who'd caused it more bitterly than ever. The king and his cursed Poynings, Black James, and, yes, even Piers, whose running abjectly to the king to plead innocence of the troubles we Fitzgeralds had caused made us all the more vulnerable. After all, if a son-in-law would show no loyalty for Father, he was destitute, indeed.

I wondered endlessly how it was I could hate and love Piers at the same time. Dimly, I remembered Mother saying something about love and hate being but extremes of the same emotion. It certainly must have been so. But I despised myself too for allowing myself to love him who'd betrayed us. I prayed I'd never see him again.

And the next moment, fell back to my knees and asked God to cancel that prayer entirely.

We lived for news of what was happening in England.

Lionel haunted the Dublin wharf, questioning all English ships for news of events there. Always it was the same. Gerait More was in the Tower awaiting the king's pleasure, who seemed gleefully content to let him cool his heels there. There'd been uncovered a Yorkist plot against the king, and many high-born Englishmen, including the brother-in-law of the king's own mother, had been arrested and executed, the latter because he purportedly said that if he were sure Perkin Warbeck were indeed Edward's son, he'd have no choice but to support him. My heart sank at this news. If the king would execute his mother's husband's own kinsman, that same Sir William Stanley who'd rescued Richard's crown from under a hawthorn bush at Bosworth field and given it to his brother to crown his Tudor stepson, what chance had Father should the king be convinced of his guilt?

But there was never any news of Piers. It was as though he were deliberately staying out of the range of notice, no doubt hoping the king would forget he was married to a Fitzgerald, I thought bitterly.

So each day dragged on in anxiety and hard work. Mother's labor began June twenty-first, midsummer day, at dawn, and culminated with the birth of a tiny, perfect girl at dusk. Weakened by the months of hunger and worry, Mother scarcely seemed aware of the new reason for her sufferings, only of the necessity to endure. But when it was over, the babe and Mother cleansed and lying together in the great bed, she roused herself enough to examine her new daughter anxiously, as if to be certain she was not harmed by her own deprivations. She kissed the exquisite little hands and cheeks, tears running down her cheeks.

"Christen her Joan for your father's mother," she whispered hoarsely. "And find some means to let your father know."

Then she drifted into a coma-like sleep, which was to be her general condition from then on.

Mother had no milk for the baby, and at first we found a village girl who'd recently given birth to a healthy boy, but soon, like Mother, weakened by the fast imposed on her early in her pregnancy, her milk too failed and we had to feed both children goat's milk from a pin-pricked bladder. Fortunately, both thrived on it.

During the summer, Perkin Warbeck, finding the hospitality of his European hosts growing strained, made an inept attempt to land at Deal in England, only to have many of his "army" captured and executed. He, himself, with the ragtag council he'd formed, escaped and attempted to land at Waterford in Ireland, where, in spite of Cousin Maurice's ill-advised attempts to raise the standard of rebellion, the citizens drove him off. He sailed away, no one knew where, but there were rumors he'd go to Scotland, for James IV, willing to do anything to annoy Henry Tudor, had offered him support. He was the only monarch left who'd not finally tired of the young man's pretensions.

When I heard of it from a messenger who'd brought Uncle Thomas' assurances that Father was still safe in the Tower and Gerry with the queen, I thought of the young man who'd called himself Richard, Duke of York, as one does a childhood friend who'd not lived up to early promise. Comely and gentle as he was, his pretensions were growing tiresome. Why didn't he drop them and go into the obscurity from which he'd sprung? Surely he realized, after what had happened to Sir William Stanley and to Father, that the king had lost patience with pretenders. His end seemed to me to be foreordained. When it no longer suited James of Scotland to annoy England's king, he'd surrender the lad as part of a peace treaty, and then, at the very least, he'd end his days in the Tower. If he was lucky enough to avoid the horrible traitor's death of hanging, drawing and quartering. Often I offered a prayer for the young man's welfare, although I felt for him now only a pitying contempt. How could I have thought I loved him? There had been no limit, it seemed, to the lengths I had been willing to pursue to escape marrying Piers. Passionately I wished I'd never heard of him; in the next instant I knew I could not bear never having known him.

I heard no word from him.

Mother grew daily weaker and touched with doom. She

seldom knew us but spoke from the depths of gentle, remembering dreams, as though she'd retreated into her own past to escape the knowledge of her bleak present. Nell, Agnes and I took turns sitting with her, for often, waking suddenly, she'd try to spring from bed as she had in the past, hurrying to see to dressing the children for Mass and breakfast, and, so weak was she, we feared she'd fall and harm herself. So, throughout the summer and fall, one or the other of us would sit by her side, coaxing her to eat a few bites or sip a little ale or water, but mostly listening in despair as she relived her past happiness, calling happily to one or the other of her children or murmuring tender words to Father.

Then, one night near the end of November, she wakened and sat up in bed, her eyes clear and bright. She stared into the shadows beyond the firelight and smiled, transforming the thin face with joy. Alone with her, I turned to stare with her at the shadows, so delighted was her cognizance that I thought someone had come into the room while I dozed.

"Gerald, dearest, have you come at last, then?" she cried, extending her arms. "Come, love, the night is cold. Let me wrap you in my hair as I used to do and we'll love each other well."

There was no one in the shadows. I turned to her with pity and would have risen to enfold her, but with a deep sigh she fell back on the pillows. Her huge eyes sought me out and tears overflowed them.

"He's not there, Magheen. Tell him . . . tell him . . . I really tried to wait. Tell him I love him . . . "

With a last gentle sigh, she slipped away from me.

There is no use speaking of my grief. It was far and away too great to put into words. And there were all the others who'd great need of my strength. I couldn't indulge myself in useless sorrow. For months I'd been acting as chatelaine of Maynooth, and now, more than ever, they all turned to me for guidance and comfort. Never have I seen such sorrow as Mother's death brought to castle and village. There'd not been man, woman or child who would not happily have died in her behalf, who'd not known her quiet, gentle kindness. More than ever, I longed to be like her and despised my Fitzgerald pride and high temper. Yet, perhaps for the first time in my life, a vague, disquieting disappointment in my deeply loved mother crept into my heart.

I would not have been so beaten down by grief that I died, I thought, even as I tried to avoid such ruminations as disloyal to her memory. But as the days of hard work continued, I came to understand that she was as she was. It had been her nature to be all things to all people, to almost *breathe* in unison with Father. At Maynooth we mourned her as if we'd lost a saint. And no one mourned her more than I, who so longed to be like her and was so very different. As I watched the grief and confusion among my family, I had to face, once and for all, that I could never, never inspire the love and devotion she had.

But, after all, where would they all have been through trouble and dearth and tragedy without prickly, strident Magheen?

There had been little shipping between England and Ireland since before Mother's death, and no way for me to get word to England had I wanted to. I had determined that I would return to England on the first ship that put in at Dublin, for I couldn't bear the thought of some hostile or indifferent jailer giving my father word that Mother had died. Accordingly, I had left word with the harbormaster that I was to be notified at Maynooth when a ship arrived from London. Late in February, a carter brought word to Maynooth that *The Porpoise* had docked at Dublin and would sail the following morning with the tide. Hurriedly, with Alice's help, I packed what I'd need and told Lionel to prepare horses for us both and have Jimmy come along to bring our mounts back to Maynooth when we'd embarked.

The carter had scarcely left when Piers came riding

from Dublin, and, recognized by the gateward, he'd been admitted to the inner bailey. When Beth came to tell me he was in the great hall, I nearly wept with joy.

But we'd parted in anger; I'd told him I'd not return to Kilkenny with him, and I wondered now why he'd come to Maynooth. *If he thought I would forget his past behavior* . . . But, perhaps he had news of Father, so, partly for that and mostly, I confess, because I couldn't wait to see him, I ran headlong down the main stairs, slowing to a more sedate pace before I came into his view at the bottom of the tower.

He was standing before the fire, warming his hands, and turned toward me as I came into the room. Good food had restored his fine looks and he was dressed in quiet magnificence, his murrey cloak lined with vair, a heavy Lancastrian collar of gold across his chest.

"You are looking well, Piers," I said with feigned coolness, just as though we'd not quarreled bitterly before he left.

"Well, you're not," he said flatly. "What the hell have you been doing with yourself? Your hair is dull . . . different, and you don't appear to have gained the flesh you lost in the siege. Your hands look as though you've been doing tanner's work."

"Complimentary, as always," I said, frowning. "If I don't look well, it's because I've not had time to care for my hands nor hair. As for the lost flesh, Poynings left precious little to eat, and what there was had to be given to the children and the sick. I've had enough, no thanks to the king's army."

"When I get you home to Kilkenny, I'll have to see that you rest and eat," he said matter-of-factly.

My heart leaped up with happy excitement that he had come with the intention of fetching me home, but, at the same time, I was angry that he chose to ignore the things I'd said to him when we'd parted.

"I *told* you I was not returning to Kilkenny," I said icily. "Thanks to your cousin, I'm needed here more than ever."

"His Royal Highness understands now how unjustly Poynings has been treating the Irish and will put a stop to it, Margaret. Indeed, he is willing to pardon your father too, if he'll but listen to reason."

"Is that true?" I said hopefully. Then, "What do you mean, 'listen to reason'?"

Piers laughed cynically. "Well, when he was first captured and brought before the king, your father was like a wild man. He told His Majesty in great detail just what he'd do to certain parts of Poynings' anatomy if they'd only unshackle him for a moment."

"Well, what did you expect him to do?" I said spiritedly but suppressing a smile.

"Knowing your father, *I* wasn't the least bit surprised by his behavior. But Henry of England is nothing if not reasonable, and he ordered your father put into the Tower until he calmed down. He told his jailer that anytime Gerait More was willing to discuss the charges against him like a reasonable man and make humble obeisance to his true king, perhaps some compromise could be agreed upon."

"And my father told him exactly what he thought of compromising with the likes of James Butler and Edward Poynings," I said, nodding.

"So, you see, Margaret, if he'll only listen to reason, which he's surely ready to do—it's been a year since he was put into the Tower—he could be coming home to your family. And your mother and grandfather can hold things together here until he does."

I stared up into his face, and the tears I'd thought I'd conquered sprang to my eyes.

"What is it, Magheen?" he said gently.

"Mother is dead, Piers," I said bleakly.

He lifted his hand in a quick, pained, ineffectual gesture and shook his head as if in denial. Then abruptly he pulled me into his arms. "Poor child, poor, poor child," he murmured and held me while the long-suppressed tears flowed.

I had not felt so at peace since he'd left. I wanted to stay there within the shelter of his arms forever. Yet a tiny voice mocked me. *He's back to make peace, now that the king is willing to pardon Gerait More. He's not afraid of guilt by association.*

I pulled away from him and stood back, wiping my eyes on the back of my hand. "So you see," I said, "I'm not going to Kilkenny with you. I am needed here. But first I have to go to England. I *have* to see Father. I will *make* the vile king let me see him! He has to be told about Mother, and I don't see how he'll bear it." I stopped suddenly, overcome as I thought of Father's grief when he heard his beloved Lady Allison had died.

"You'll do better if you curb your temper, Margaret," Piers said expressionlessly. "His Highness has had about enough Fitzgerald tantrums."

"Don't be criticizing us for having tantrums," I cried. "It's all the Butlers' fault in the first place."

"As always, I am fascinated by your process of reasoning," he drawled. "But there's no use going into that; we'll never agree anyhow. Some people only learn the hard way. I would never have believed it would take a year in the Tower before your father would listen to reason. His guard reports he's as vehement as ever."

"Well, the news that Poynings has indirectly caused the death of his countess will knock the fight out of him, no doubt," I said bitterly.

He was silent for a long moment. "When are you leaving for London, Margaret?" he said at last.

"On the ship that apparently brought you. On the morning tide," I said expressionlessly.

"Go to the queen," he said suddenly. "She is a kind and gentle lady and has as much influence with Henry as anyone, now that his uncle is dead. Well, except for his mother, who is as determined to have things her way as her son," he added with a smile. "Yet Henry pleases Queen Elizabeth when he can, and he's not unkind himself. He may grant you leave to visit your father."

I thanked him grudgingly.

"Will you, then, when you've seen him, return to Ireland?" he asked casually.

"Aye, unless there's something I can do for him there. Ireland is my home."

"Kilkenny is your home. I think you should come back to it when things are settled here."

But my pride wouldn't let me tell him how I longed to return to Kilkenny with him. He'd not done what I wanted, and neither would I give him the satisfaction of doing what he wanted. "I *am* at home," I insisted. "This is where I'm wanted and needed."

He sighed deeply. "You are a spoiled brat, Margaret Fitzgerald, and I'm giving you fair warning, I'll not ask you again. Now, will you return to Kilkenny when you get back?"

"Don't you issue ultimatums to me, Piers Butler," I cried. "You left me to cope as best I could just so you could curry favor with the king, and I've not the slightest mind to obey your wishes now."

"Then, let whatever happens between us be on your own head."

And without waiting for my answer, he turned and left Maynooth without looking back.

I took a step to follow him, suddenly frightened that *this* time he really would abandon me. But bad as was my fear of losing him, the old, familiar Fitzgerald pride was greater. Butlers! His family and the other cursed Lancastrians had caused all this. I wish I'd never seen any of them.

But my heart ached as I prepared to ride to Dublin. For all I knew, he might start annulment or divorce proceedings. With Father in disgrace, there was no longer any reason for Butler to unite with Fitzgerald to please the king. Being the sensible man he was, Piers would have seen the wisdom of having our marriage dissolved. Like as not he was already considering some other maid the king had suggested, some noblewoman unconnected with the fallen fortunes of Kildare.

But it was no time for self-pity and I disdained to indulge in it.

In London we inquired where the queen then lodged and was told she'd retired to Sheen, her favorite castle, which had been her childhood home. The king was with her and they comforted each other, it was said, for the deaths of his uncle Jasper, who'd kept him safe during all the years the Yorkists were in power and had been his principal adviser after he was crowned, and for the little Princess Elizabeth, who'd died very suddenly the previous September. Even the dread Lancastrians were not immune to losing their loved ones, I thought, and drew a certain reassurance thereby. Surely, no matter how Father had angered him, the king would grant me permission to be the one to take Father the terrible news of Mother's death.

We hired a boat to row us upriver, staring wonderingly at the great bridge with shops all along either length so that it seemed a castle wing extended over the river, the somber Tower of London, huge and brooding as if in satisfaction at having concealed my father within its mysterious walls, at the cranes and fine ships, great manor houses and castles that crowded down to the river's edge. We rounded a bend in the river and the oarsman pointed out Westminster Palace and Abbey, busy as a small town although the king was absent, and finally, after passing many a fine house and budding field, we came to the dock at Sheen.

I sent a message to Uncle Thomas, begging the man-at-arms who guarded the gate to have it carried. When I'd given him a handful of silver coins, he bellowed for a page and, in a moment, my own brother, grown leggy and awkward but handsome and sweet-faced as ever, came trotting through the gate.

"Gerry, oh Gerry, darling!" I screamed, gathering him into my arms.

"Magheen? It isn't you, Magheen?" he gasped, clamping a bear hug around my ribs that made them ache. "Oh,

Magheen, by Saint Bride, I've missed you so. How came
you here? How's Mother?"

He stopped short as he released me enough to see my
face.

"What's amiss, Magheen?"

"Gerry, love, you've had to be a man far beyond your
years so far, and so must you continue to be," I said, taking
his hands in mine.

"Has . . . has the king executed Father? I thought he'd
not . . ." he cried.

"Not Father, darling. It's Mother, Gerry. Mother is
dead."

He collapsed into my arms in wracking sobs. Manly as
his bearing had been throughout, he was only a heart-
broken little boy now. He clung to me, burrowing his face
into my neck, clenching and unclenching his outsize, boy's
hands in my cloak. I had dreaded telling Father so much
I'd not thought greatly about how poor little Gerry would
react. Pityingly, I held him close. We other children had
had each other. I thanked God now that I had come for
Gerry's sake. Could telling Father be any worse than this
racking sorrow my homesick little brother was suffering? I
bent my head over his, biting my lips to keep from explod-
ing in fury that this travail had come to us. It was the
Lancastrians, none other, who were to blame. Black
James, to be sure; but the cursed Lancastrian king and his
followers had brought this trouble to us.

At last Gerry subsided a little and the man-at-arms,
who'd been watching us with pitying interest, I thought,
nodded brusquely to indicate we should all step into the
outer courtyard.

"Are you better now, Gerry?" I said softly, offering him
my handkerchief.

He nodded, gulping and blinking rapidly at the ocean of
tears. I held him against my side and he leaned against me
gratefully. "What . . . why did Mother die, Magheen?" he
said at last.

"For grief, pure and simple," Lionel burst out, snuffing

and mopping at his eyes with the back of his hands. "Grief, lad, for your father and y'rself."

I stared at him silently. I supposed he was right, for, though of course the siege and her confinement had weakened her, it was her retreat from reality, the black mourning depression brought on by Father and Gerry's dilemma, that had killed her.

"She left us another sister, Gerry," I said gently. "Had word of that reached you?"

"Aye, Magheen. Piers's Uncle Thomas gives me your letters to read, though, technically, I'm a hostage and not entitled to be treated so well."

"*Do* they treat you well, Gerry?"

"Aye, I can't complain, Magheen, though I've not been allowed to see Father."

I shifted my reticule into my other hand, and Lionel, seeing it was heavy for me, took it himself. I told him to wait for us in the courtyard and walked along beside my little brother.

"Gerry, what is the queen like?" I asked as we reached the palace steps. "Do you think she might be able to get the king to allow me to take word of Mother's death to Father?"

He considered for a moment. "He might. He listens to any request, but he does what pleases him. The Duke of Bedford, that is, his Uncle Jasper, who died last year, had the most influence with him. The Lady Margaret Beaufort, his mother, pesters him a lot. The queen doesn't. But he will do things she and his mother ask him to if it's of small moment."

I nodded. His assessment seemed to agree with Piers's.

"Come, we'll go to see her right now," Gerry said.

"Can you go in like that? Without being summoned?"

"Aye. The old courtiers say she's like her father in that way. He used to be most kind and friendly with even the lowest of his subjects. Folk like her better than the king."

I did not wonder when I'd met them both.

We left Lionel waiting in the anteroom and Gerry drew

me into the queen's own bower, proudly announcing to the ladies surrounding her that I was his sister. She was very pretty, with pink and white skin and wide, sky-blue eyes, and, when Gerry had told her who I was and why I'd come to court, her soft face collapsed in genuine pity. When she spoke, there was that about her voice and manner that reminded me a little of Mother, although she was little older than myself.

"Lady Margaret, I am truly sorry," she said earnestly. "My father spoke often of your parents. He said your mother was the most beautiful woman in Ireland, and if you look at all like her I can understand why."

I thanked her haltingly, grateful for the ease with which she spoke to me.

"I am grateful that I got to England first with the news, Your Grace," I said with a catch in my voice. "I . . . I . . . wanted to be the one to tell my father and Gerry, here. Such news ought not to come from a jailer, or, in Gerry's case, from a guardian, no matter how kind."

"Well-spoken, Lady Margaret. I agree. Therefore, would you like me to ask the king to give you a passport to see your father?"

"I prayed you would, Your Grace."

She put her needlework into the hands of one of her attendants and stood up, straightening her gown. She was taller than I, with broad shoulders but amazingly dainty feet and hands. She put her arm around my shoulder and walked with me toward the door of her room.

"He's working on the accounts now. I fear he works far too hard, insisting on checking the treasurer's books and, indeed, every bit of business conducted in this realm." She sighed as if in resignation. "My father was like that," she continued reminiscently, "but he took more time to enjoy life. I am glad my husband has the good of the realm so much at heart. Forgive me, child, you can have little interest in all this. We'll go to the king this very minute and I know he'll give you leave."

"You are so kind, Your Grace, I thank you from the bottom of my heart." Then, hesitantly, encouraged by her friendly way, "Have you . . . have you any idea what will become of my father?"

Gerry's face relaxed a little and the queen smiled.

"I suppose I shouldn't tell you this, but he's to be given a chance to answer the charges against him soon. My husband has talked to him before, but he was so outraged, so vehement in his protestations of complete innocence . . . to the extent, my child, that he struck one of his guards so hard he knocked him unconscious, that Henry ordered him confined a while longer . . . to sweat the rebelliousness out of him, he says."

"He *is* innocent, Your Grace."

"Your brother keeps telling me so," she laughed. "Here, we're at the king's door; you tell him."

She said a word to the guard in the Tudor livery of green and white, and the door opened at his command.

The king was seated at a long table, a stack of accounts lying in front of him. A priest and several splendidly dressed courtiers stood about anxiously while a tiny woman in a gown almost nun-like in its severity sat beside and a little behind him knitting contentedly. The queen presented me to him and to the little woman, Lady Margaret Beaufort, the king's mother.

He was not in the least what I'd expected.

Tired gray eyes looked out of a long, almost emaciated face, and the expression in them seemed perpetually cynical. Yet, when the queen told him who I was, he laughed appealingly and rose to welcome me. The laugh had never reached his eyes, however much he smiled. He was no taller than the queen, very slender with long, small bones. His clothing was magnificent green cloth-of-gold but shabby, and the leather shoes that stuck out beneath the hem of the long robe were decidedly scuffed with wear. His fingers were as ink-stained as any clerk's, and the foolscap he'd been using to double-check his figures was covered to the last tiny margin with small, fine columns as if he couldn't bear to waste any scrap of paper. Men said he could account for every penny spent in the entire country; obviously they did not exaggerate.

I curtsyed deeply, a little unnerved that he had stood, although, in truth, I'd never met a king before and didn't really know but what such a courtesy was commonplace among royalty. He was obviously as penurious of his time as of his money, for he made an impatient motion for me to speak.

"I . . . I want to thank Your . . . Your Majesty," I stammered over the new royal title he was known to favor over "Your Grace," "for receiving me so graciously." I hated the conciliatory sound of my own voice. More than anything on earth, I wanted to spit in the Tudor's eye, yet that would get me nothing but a room in the Tower near Father, no doubt, and he'd be worse off than before.

"Yes, it's all right, Lady Margaret," he said a bit peevishly. "What is it you want of me?"

"To see my father, Your Majesty," I continued humbly.

"You're aware he's still in the Tower, under my deep displeasure. Answerable for treasonous acts against the Crown?" he said shortly.

"Your Majesty, my father has not acted treasonously," I said with spirit, then checked myself quickly. "Forgive me, Your Majesty, but you have been listening to the lies of his enemies," I began again. "By having you remove my father from his post governing Ireland, which he's done these long, long years justly and well, I might add, they've had a free field to ravage Ireland at will."

I thought I detected a twinkle in the tired, gray eyes.

"I have heard that theme before, from your father and . . . others," he said wryly.

"It's true, Your Majesty. You would have only to ask any of the Irish chiefs as well as the Anglo-Irish barons. There is no one, not even your fierce Poynings, who can keep Ireland in order but my father. As for the charges that he backed Warbeck and was plotting to kill Poynings, surely you have considered the source. 'Tis said in Ireland that you are finally learning the caliber of Sir James Butler and have banished him from court."

He laughed and shook his head. "The maid's as audacious as her father," he cried.

"Forgive me, Your Majesty, I did not mean to harangue you about the charges against him," I said, forcing myself to speak abjectly. "I have come only to beg permission to see my father for a few minutes. You may send armed guards along if you fear I would slip him a weapon or a rope or some means of escape, only let me talk to him."

"Please let her, Henry. She's come to England with the news that her mother is dead," the queen interjected.

The thin eyebrows raised in sudden surprise. "I didn't know, Lady Margaret. I'm sorry for you, poor child, but I have given orders he's to be held in solitary confinement with no visitors. The sooner to bring him to his senses, indeed."

"Your mother recently bore a child, did she not?" Lady Beaufort said suddenly.

"Aye, milady, on Midsummer Day," I said politely.

"Then she didn't die in childbirth?"

"Nay, but she'd been much weakened by childbirth and . . ."—I stole a glance at the king—". . . by hunger when Sir Edward Poynings held Maynooth in siege."

The king had the grace to look uncomfortable.

"I well remember my own confinement with you after your poor father had died in the cause of Lancaster, Henry," the little sharp-faced woman said. "I suffered greatly, being only thirteen, and the physicians said it was because of my youth and the worry that I never grew more. 'Twas a sad, bleak time for me, bringing forth England's hope alone, struck with grief from the loss of your father. Rebel though he is, it seems unmerciful to deny the girl permission to tell Fitzgerald of his wife's death."

Queen Elizabeth look startled, as if she was not used to having the king's mother side with her.

The king stared at me moodily. "It might be a good idea

at that to allow his lass to take him the word. Let him see
how sore needed he is at home. I think he knows by now
he'll never go there again except by my grace."

Lady Margaret nodded approvingly. "How wise you
are, Henry. How like you to turn it to your advantage,"
she said with satisfaction.

I struggled to hide my distaste of the two of them. The
queen threw me a sad, whimsical little smile that seemed
to show she understood and sympathized. I realized suddenly with a flash of intuition that the queen suffered
greatly and silently. She seemed to care deeply about her
husband. How terrible it must have been for her to watch
him subdue her father's old friends. I wondered how she
could stand the constant turmoil over the string of pretenders. Surely she must often question if any of them
were truly her little brother. I understood entirely the tearing of loyalties she must have felt, for I too had come to
love my enemy. At least her Henry seemed to reciprocate
her feelings, which was more than I could say of Piers.
Resolutely I pushed the thought of him away; Father was
my main care now.

"You may go to him, Lady Margaret," the king said at
last. "I'll have a passport with my seal readied and, if your
bargeman has gone, the royal barge to carry you down to
the Tower."

I could not restrain a wide smile. That it was the first
time I'd smiled in weeks I was painfully aware when my
stiff, dry lips cracked. I dabbed at the drop of blood I felt,
and then at my eyes, which filled with unexpected tears of
relief. Though I resented the sparse little king deeply, feeling none of these tragedies would have befallen us in the
first place but for him, I was overwhelmed with gratitude
that he'd allowed my request.

He gazed down at me thoughtfully. "Tell your sire I
pray, for his sake, that the counsel he chooses is as fervent
in his defense as you are. I will hear his case when he is
ready. It's entirely up to him now."

I thanked him sincerely and went down on my knees to kiss the proffered hand.

It tasted of ink.

Three paces to and three paces back. Step two paces, turn on the third. Step two paces, turn on the third.

I gazed into the tiny cell through the grill in the heavy door, observing my poor father unseen while the jailer fumbled for the key. When at last it turned in the lock, Father looked up from his pacing as though startled by the sound, which, indeed, he likely was if no visitors had been allowed him in the year he'd spent imprisoned. He gazed unseeingly in the lightless hole, seeming to be blinded by the rushlight the turnkey carried. Impatiently I thrust a coin in payment into the man's hand and took the lamp from him, placing it on an outjutting stone.

"He's not to have lights," he said, but the coin disappeared into his dirty clothes, nonetheless.

"He'll have lights now, you villain, and a charcoal brazier too," I said indignantly.

"Things like that cost money."

"I've money. Go see to it this minute. Food too. And another blanket."

He locked the door behind me and went off with Lionel to bring what I'd ordered.

"Lionel, see he doesn't cheat us," I warned. "And do you try not to buy London Bridge."

Father blinked and sank down on the reeking cell's only furniture, a three-legged stool. He was nearly as thin as Henry Tudor!

"By Saint Bride, I think my mind's playing tricks again," he muttered thickly. He shook his head and I saw a louse drop loose and fall to the wet floor. My feet felt cold as an Englishman's heart even through my fur-lined boots, and I saw with pity that Father's feet were nearly bare, for his boots had rotted away in the damp.

"Your mind's all right, dear; it's me, Magheen," I said, sinking down to embrace him.

He drew back as if still not trusting his senses, and stared at me owlishly.

"Magheen?" he croaked, running a filthy hand along my cheek and staring with wonder at the tears he found there. "How come you to be here, lass?"

"To see you, Father. To talk to you." I tried to control my quavering voice, the pity in my heart. He was so changed! I had not seen him for three years and I would not have known him. The high-hearted, handsome, twinkling-eyed warrior that I remembered was an uncertain, gray-bearded, middle-aged man, sick and forlorn. As if seeing my shocked despair, he made an ineffectual motion along his thin form. "A fine sight I am to see, lass, with naught for company but lice and cold." Then, as if finally aware it was truly me, he threw his arms around me joyfully and enfolded me in thin but still powerful arms. "God be praised, Magheen," he said with a catch in his throat.

At last he released me and held me at arm's length. "I should not have grabbed you, Daughter. You'll be leaving here with enough livestock to pollute every rover in England."

"Don't worry, Father, I've money for a bath. And enough to buy you coals and rushes and blankets too," I said, wanting to offer him some comforting before telling him my sad news.

"So, I've another fair daughter, lass," he said. "That's the last I've heard of home, and 'tis the lack of news that troubles me the most. "I even heard your mother named her Joan. But how did she fare, Magheen? She is not young for breeding."

I could not meet his eyes. But I took his big cold hands between my own, pressing them, willing my sympathy and love into them.

"Father, I would give my own life if I could tell you other. But she is dead, Father."

My most terrible imaginings didn't prepare me for the white horror in his face. He stared at me dumbly for a long moment, and the only sound was my own nervous breathing. Then he whirled up and away and beat with his fists against the rough stone wall, and the howl that came from his throat would have made a banshee blanch and cross himself. I could do nothing but wait until the worst was over and he'd slumped against the wall. Then did I get up from my knees and go to stand beside him, my arms around his defeated form as far as they'd reach. Never could I have supposed this near collapse, for it was all my strength could do to hold him erect. I realized suddenly that I'd wanted to come to London for myself as well as for him. I'd held my own grief in abeyance through these long weeks because they needed my strength at Maynooth. And in my deepest heart I'd thought, when I reached the comfort of Father's arms I'd be able to let go, that we could comfort each other for our great loss. The total defeat of him showed me he had no strength to spare for me.

"What shall I ever do without her? She is the heart that beats in my body. Without her I can only wither and die."

His words frightened me beyond measure. I grasped his shoulders and stood back, shaking him a little to make him look at me. "Don't say that, Father. We've been through too much to lose you too. We all need you. Ireland needs you."

He shook his head stupidly, despair in every movement.

"'Tis not that I don't love you . . . God knows I do. Ireland too, like my own mother, God grant her peace. But without Allison I have no heart for anything. I have been ill with longing for her, yet I could think of her safe at Maynooth, biding and praying for me. I never doubted that in the king's good time I'd be returning to her arms. What have I to give anyone without your mother behind me?"

"You must pull yourself together now, Father. The king bade me tell you he's ready to hear your defense anytime you're willing to appear before him."

He sank down onto the stool again, his head in his

hands, moaning softly. "I can't defend myself now. I don't care what happens to me. Let him send me to the block for all I care."

"Father! I'm ashamed of you," I cried. "And what would Mother say to such an attitude?"

"Your poor, poor mother," he continued in the same mournful monotone. "Sorry the day she met me."

"Sorry? Father, that is not what I gathered from her last days. Her heart was broken by your troubles, it's true, but only because the love she bore you was so great. She was so happy with you, Father, she would rather not have been born than missed being your wife, and so she kept saying all those last months. Indeed, Father, she should have died when Joannie was born in June, but she held on for you by sheer will, and when she hadn't the strength to hold any longer, she said, 'Tell Gerald I tried to wait, tell him I love him.'" I took his bearded chin and forced his face up so that he had to meet my eyes. "Her last words were of you, Father. You know she'll not even leave the gates of heaven for its glories until we all arrive. You cannot so lose faith with her that you'd droop and pine like a maid."

"You don't understand, Magheen. We were . . . when a man and woman love as we did, they are truly one entity. You are asking me to go on as a half. Perhaps it's my punishment that you don't understand. I made you marry Piers, whom you didn't love . . . I . . . I beg your pardon, darling, now I know what I have done."

I stared at him helplessly. Always he had been the one who was boisterous, in charge of everything. The strong fortress that had sheltered us all. Mother had seemed to us a gentle wraith whom Father had cossetted and kissed or railed at and bullied. I had not suspected that she was the real strength of our home. And of Gerait More. Desperately I searched my heart for some way to snap him out of his apathetic grief. What had Mother done to get him to do what she wanted? I forced myself to remember her quiet ways. She'd always been calmly steadfast, standing by her principles when Father would have bullied her, managing to hold her own without fuss, whereas I, though much like her in my principles, tended to shout the walls down to get my way. Thinking of that, willing myself to serenity, I changed my tactics.

"Father, I have been at Maynooth since you were taken," I said. "Piers is God knows where, not where he'd do *me* any good, that's for sure. And Black James continues to pillage and rape all over Ireland. He swore he'd have me too, Father."

"He said that?"

"Aye. He said it was his destiny to have me and would have raped me the day they took Gerry but for Poynings. And when you speak of evil, Father, there's another. Why, he threatened to make a catamite of Gerry. Fortunately, for now, Gerry's with the queen, but if you should be executed for treason . . ."

"Goddamned whoreson cursed . . ." That was only the beginning of the curses, mostly in Gaelic. I stared at him admiringly. He sounded almost like the old Gerait More. He came up off the stool, kicking it violently against the wall, and went to the door to bawl for the jailer.

"I want paper and pen," he shouted. "I want to write a letter for my daughter to carry to the king."

And when I left the Tower I had Father's abject request to answer to the charges of treason and his promise not to rant and rail in court.

CHAPTER 7

True to his word, King Henry summoned Father to stand before him to answer charges before the week was out.

The queen had gotten permission for me to watch from the shelter of a pillar in one of the galleries, and Gerry was allowed to accompany me to the Star Chamber of Westminster Palace where the trial was to be held. Arriving early, we watched the king, his entire council, and Father's accusers arrive. Gerry pointed them out to me, identifying them by name, for, in his quick way, he'd become familiar with all of them and chattered tidbits of court gossip about each as they appeared. No one paid any attention to pages, he said, as if in explanation of his knowing so much about court matters, and spoke freely in front of them.

I knew the Irish prelates who'd come to court to accuse Father, of course. Always Father had been the bane of the bishops, a veritable thorn in their sides, for he accused them consistently and vociferously of being self-serving and dissolute as well as strangers to the spirit of Christ's laws. His assessment was not far wrong in most cases; the bishops generally oppressed the laity and the poor clergy in their jurisdiction as mercilessly as some of the barons misused their serfs and tenants. Many had been the time one or the other of them had threatened Father with excommunication, but he'd just laughed and declared that the day he was excommunicated he'd go in person to Rome with such true tales, proof provided gratis, of their depredations behind the protection of the cloth that the Holy Father would have them cleaning the castle pits in the Vatican. It was little wonder, therefore, now that Father was in trouble with the King of England, that so many of them had come to appear against him. There was Archbishop Walter Fitzsimmonds, the prelate at Dublin, who'd married Piers and me, smug and sleek in silken clothing that looked most unecclesiastical, Octavian de Palatio, the Bishop of Armaugh, a tall, swarthy Italian who'd pretended to support the Simnel lad in 1486, then, after learning of the coronation plans, deserting the Yorkists and going to England to betray those who'd trusted him, and, the one Father hated most of all, John Payne, Bishop of Meath, who'd actually been the one to explain and confirm Simnel's right to the throne and, with his own hands, had taken the golden crown from the statue of the Virgin to crown the pretend Earl of Warwick with. Yet he'd told the king it was all Father's and Uncle Maurice's doing and he'd been forced at sword point to take part in the mockery of a coronation. He was a mountain of a man, both in stature and in girth, bald well beyond his tonsure, with watery blue eyes that darted shrewdly and missed nothing, and an intimidating, booming bass voice. Apparently, the bishops had chosen him as spokesman and prosecutor, for he sat well in the forefront, opposite the stool Father was to take.

I'd had limited funds to work with, but I'd managed to buy Father a new doublet and hose of murrey discreetly trimmed with tiny bands of fur and a decent pair of shoes, for the Irish garb I'd brought along had been so big it hung on his gaunt frame. It had seemed a discreet move anyhow for him to wear the English clothing Poynings' hated statutes had commanded, and when Father strode proudly into the courtroom I realized my instincts had been right, for, thin though he was, he was far and away the handsomest man in the chamber. Lionel had outdone himself bathing him, barbering the shaggy head and shaving his face in the English fashion. His eyes glittered feverishly handsome under neatly trimmed eyebrows, and the gray of his hair only made them the bluer and more magnetic.

When he'd taken his place, the king, splendid in black

velvet with a Lancastrian collar of gold and rubies about his neck, smiled bleakly and leaned forward, making a steeple out of his thin fingers.

"I think we may dispense with the formalities of a court," he said with a silencing glance at the row of bishops. "I believe, Milord of Kildare, you are ready to contain yourself and answer with decorum the charges of treason brought by your countrymen."

I could see Father's throat work slightly and the big hands tense infinitesimally, but he had himself firmly in hand and answered temperately.

"Aye, Your Majesty, I apologize for my past vehemence and humbly submit myself to your judgment."

The king nodded approvingly.

"Then you are willing to accept as prosecutor His Grace of Meath?"

"One bishop's much like another," Father said with a small twinkle and bowed toward Payne. "'Tis good to meet you again, Your Grace," he added mildly.

"Is it, then, you murdering gallowglass," the Bishop snapped, obviously annoyed by the small titter running through the court at Father's ambiguous remark. "Strange to hear you say such a thing considering that last time we met, just before My Lord Poynings captured you, you and your men killed my companion Lord Plunkett, and would have me, I've no doubt, had I not escaped you."

"Aye, I remember," Father said, seeming to ponder a moment, "'twas after your force of twenty ambushed my twelve, was it not, Milord Bishop? And you *did* disappear with great facility; indeed, our horses, being much wearied, could not begin to overtake your lightning retreat."

The courtroom was like an audience at a comedy, suppressing guffaws and buzzing to one another. Father kept his face immobile, but Gerry punched me and whispered, "Look at the laughing eyes of him."

The bishop glared furiously, sputtering. Father took advantage of his discomposure to turn toward the king.

"Your Majesty, I admit to many actions that may have seemed rebellious on the surface, but, when I have been allowed to acquaint you with the extenuating circumstances, you'll understand I meant no treason. However, having been appointed no counsel, I know not how to best present my case before you."

The king was silent a moment, smiling his curiously mirthless smile, his eyes inscrutable. Yet, I felt, he seemed inclined to goodwill toward my father and proved it when he spoke.

"I have no intention that you should be tried without counsel, Fitzgerald. You should know by now that there is justice for all in England. My council is filled with many learned men, well-versed in ecclesiastical and civil law. You may choose from among them. Indeed, if you deem them too partial, being my own advisers, you may choose from any man in England and I will have him brought to you."

"Spoken most fairly, Your Majesty, and I am much impressed. And gratified," Father said. Then he sighed and looked up with a wry smile. "I have no doubt you mean what you say, but I must respectfully point out that I doubt very much you'll let me have the good fellow I would choose."

"By my truth and oath, I shall."

"And would you give me your hand on that?"

"Here it is, milord." To the court's amazement, Henry got up and advanced to the dock and thrust his slender hand into Father's great, chilblained mitt. His eyes, dropping their inscrutable expression, snapped with delight at Father's disarming manner, and the court, with the exception of the bishops, seeing the king smile, rippled with chuckles. The bloc of clergy glared and seethed.

"Well, then," said the king, returning to his place, "when will you choose this counsel?"

"Never, if you leave it to him," interjected the Bishop of Meath waspishly.

Father turned back to face him, not allowing his annoyance to remove the confident smile the king's protestation of good faith had placed on his lean face.

"You lie, Bald Bishop, I'll choose now, as quickly as you would choose a fair wench, and we all know how hurriedly *that* would be."

"What is he trying to do?" I whispered, clenching my fists. "He'll be having himself thrown back into the Tower yet."

"No, Magheen, listen to them. Never did this hall hear the like," Gerry said with soft admiration.

The hall was roaring with laughter. Even the staid Lords of the exchequer were doubling over, clutching their sides. I saw with growing hope that even the English clergy among them, Richard Fox and Reginald Bray particularly, were laughing as heartily as the others.

"You accuse Milord Bishop of most unseemly conduct," Henry said with an air of urging Father on, which was obviously not lost on our sire.

"'Unseemly' is an overly kind word, Your Majesty; you'd not believe the tales I could tell on this fat bishop."

"I should like to hear one of them," Henry said, enjoying himself immensely.

"Well, then, I chanced to be walking outside his church one evening when a wondrous fair lass holding a small baby to her bosom came bursting out of the church with His Grace of Meath in hot pursuit . . ."

"He lies, Your Majesty, pay him no heed!" Payne sputtered, his face darker than Father's new doublet.

"By Saint Bride, I swear every word is true," Father said solemnly.

"Then continue, milord," said the king, steepling his fingers and leaning back.

"Well, Your Majesty, I gathered from the girl's shouted accusations that she'd found a babe beneath her belt, put there by her honest, pledged young man, but before he could marry her he'd been killed in one of that murdering bastard Sir James Butler's many sneaking raids." Father paused and threw a shrewd look toward the king, who'd not missed the reference to Father's archenemy's lawless behavior. "The girl had gone to the bishop to make a confession of her sin, which was, I'm sure, a small enough one, since the common folk tend to look on a betrothal as so nigh marriage it isn't worth differentiating. Anyhow, it seemed, yon bishop had told the lass he'd not give her absolution until she went back into the sacristy with him and . . ."

"A lie! A damned, Geraldine lie," the bishop roared. "Kildare, this time you've gone too far. I'll have you excommunicated. You'll land in hellfire!"

"Exactly what he told the maid if she didn't do as he said," Father said complacently, folding his arms across his chest. "Her answer wasn't half bad either," he mused. "She said, 'I'd rather be in hellfire if going to heaven means I have to flee a pack o' shorn bishops till the Judgment Day.' And she shifted her baby onto her other arm and stalked off down the cobbles."

The king laughed until tears ran down his cheeks, more amused, I thought, by the purpling anger of the bishop, who had no defense, since it was common knowledge he had more children than Father. At last, gaining control of himself, he motioned the court to more decorum.

"Welladay. This counsel you choose will have his work cut out for him, but I suppose you'd best choose and we'll get on with the proceeding," he said at last.

"I'll do it, Your Majesty. I am a simple man, it's true. But I know that I could search the realm and choose no better than one who's here in this courtroom."

"And that is?"

"By Saint Bride, it's you, Your Majesty," Father said triumphantly.

The king nearly fell off his throne at the sheer audacity.

"He's gone too far, Gerry," I hissed. But apparently he hadn't, for Henry was laughing uproariously, and when his council saw that he was not offended, they too howled and stomped in delight.

"You may call yourself simple, my friend, but a much

wiser man than you pretend to be might have chosen worse," Henry gasped. He stared up at Father as if reassessing him. No doubt he'd been thinking Father some dull, cloddish Irish chieftain, which was the impression he well knew how to make when it seemed profitable to do so. Though he was playing the buffoon for the court, even I, who knew his shrewd mind so well, stared in admiration at the fine footwork of choosing the king as his counsel.

But the Bishop of Meath was in a fury. "How dare you use such subterfuge in this august court," he stormed. "You are letting him use mockery and laughter to avoid paying the penalty for his many sins. What reason can he possibly give for plotting to kill Poynings, your own deputy?"

"By Saint Bride, Your Majesty, I swear on my honor I never so plotted. I went on expedition with your deputy and tried only to reason with him, telling him the rumors of myself and my friends sheltering Warbeck during that time were nonsense. So far as I know, he hadn't come near Ireland until long after I had been put in the Tower, and that I heard only from my servant or I'd not have known it. The only testimony you ever had that I plotted murder was from Sir James Butler, and we all know how trustworthy *he* is."

This brought a knowing laugh from the spectators, for the most disinterested among them knew that James had been knighted early in the Tudor reign for informing against the Yorkists in Ireland and had done nothing since then not calculated to further his campaign for legitimization and gaining control of the Ormonde lands. He had lied about Piers as readily as about Father to obtain his heart's desire, too.

"Well, you can't deny you backed the organ-maker's son," the bishop snapped, losing ground and obviously flustered.

"As many another, yourself included, did," came the bland reply.

"I thought he was the Earl of Warwick," Payne cried defensively.

"As did I," Father answered, unperturbed. Then, turning again to the king, "Your Majesty, I've been a year in your Tower of London," he continued humbly, "and I've had much time for thinking. It's very true that I was not always as true a subject as you've a right to expect. The Geraldines of Ireland had ever been Yorkists during the strife between the two houses. I loved King Edward, your own father-in-law, well, though I can't say much for his brother Richard. We believed he, Gloucester, had destroyed Edward's sons, and though we deplored his machinations and character, he *was* then the heir to the throne. Still, tyrant that he was, none of mine joined him against you when you invaded. When we did raise the standard against you, it was because we thought the child we had was truly Edward of Warwick.

"You proved beyond a doubt that he was not. Moreover, I was shown the real Earl of Warwick in the Tower and know that he, poor lad, could not govern a school of fishes, let alone England. Nor does common sense tell me that Richard ever allowed Edward's sons to live long enough to escape him, as the Warbeck lad claims to have done. No, Your Grace, I realize that you alone are King of England. Moreover, you have dealt most fairly and wisely with both Lancaster and York by taking the Princess Elizabeth as your wife. You have governed England most wisely these ten years, and I perceive that you'd do the same in Ireland could you but find a loyal deputy. I have confounded you in the past, but, by Saint Bride, if you'll give me another chance, I swear I'll not plot against you again, nor will I allow any pretender to harass you from Ireland."

The council chamber had grown very still. I stared around at the rows of solemn faces. Despite Father's humorous manner at the outset of the hearing, I could see that there was none among the king's councilors who was not favorably impressed with his honest speech. I felt myself relax a little.

"I believe you, Fitzgerald," the king said simply. "Come here, therefore, and take my hand in friendship."

The Bishop of Meath let out angry sounds.

"Your Majesty. Surely you are too wise to fall under the famous Gerait More charm," he cried stridently. "There are more charges against him . . . the . . . ask him about the burning of the cathedral at Cashel. Only ask him. He purports to be so truthful. Then let him deny that he burned the cathedral on his last rampage through the Pale after he and his father-in-law were removed as deputy and treasurer."

But the king was already won over to Father's side. He turned toward the dock, smiling indulgently. "*Did* you burn down the cathedral, milord?" he asked, already knowing that Father had.

"Aye, Your Majesty, but, you see, I thought the Bishop was inside," was the imperturbable answer.

It was many minutes before order was restored. The Bishop of Meath, shaking with anger, kept trying to speak.

"Your Majesty, Your Majesty, he's an audacious, ungovernable rogue. All Ireland cannot rule him . . ." he shouted above the laughter.

"Then," said the king, eyes dancing, "I shall set him to rule all Ireland."

And, despite the indignation of the disgruntled prelates, that was that. When Father left the courtroom, it was as the restored Deputy of Ireland.

Father was not able to return to Ireland with Lionel and me, though; there were many points to be worked out in the peace treaty the king insisted upon between Father and the Butlers. Piers was to be called to England as deputy to the Earl of Ormonde and, to my indignation, Sir James Butler as well. Not wanting to encounter either of them, and, in truth, worrying somewhat about conditions at Maynooth, Grandfather's health in particular, I took ship for home on Lady Day, March 25.

To say there was joy at Maynooth when I brought the word of Father's vindication and restoration to his post was at once an understatement and an exaggeration. Everywhere the news traveled throughout Meath there was jubilation quickly followed by tears of sorrow that the Countess of Kildare was not alive to welcome home her lord. Still, there was a feeling of well-being in the air that Ireland had not known for many a long day. The troubles were ending. Father would soon be riding at the head of the Guild again, and the Irish lords would have to stop their demands for black rent. There would be peace and prosperity again.

To be sure, Henry, though suitably impressed with Father's loyalty now, would still have young Gerry in his custody. But, then, he would have been sent to England by now to begin his education at any rate, and I, for one, after meeting the queen, knew Gerry would be in good hands nor would he be in any danger from King Henry. So the news I brought to Maynooth was only good.

Grandfather was ill indeed, despite his protestations that he was only "a little tired." Yet he insisted that the household be organized to return to Saint Thomas Court. When Father arrived from England, for a certainty, he'd have to remain in Dublin for a time; there would be much to be done to right the chaos the three years since his first removal had made of Irish affairs. So, though he was forced to ride part of the way in a litter with the little ones, early in April we returned to Dublin to await Father's arrival.

Grandfather spent an hour or two in feverish activity getting preliminary paperwork done, then took to his bed for the rest of the day. He could no longer hide the fact that he was very ill. A canker had developed in his mouth which hurt more than he'd admit, and the potion our physician gave him for the pain caused him to sleep a good deal.

Father wrote that there were still matters in England

which required his attention and that he'd be home as soon as possible. Grandfather worried that the king would not honor his promise to restore Father, that he did not, in fact, trust Father and so was delaying his return. Privately, I thought he could not bear the thought of returning to a home without Mother smiling welcome and so was delaying the sad time of truly realizing her absence. And, of course, there was likely to be some disagreement in the terms of the treaty, given such long and bitter enemies as the Butlers and the Fitzgeralds. I supposed Piers was in England; certainly *I* hadn't seen him.

With Agnes and Nell's help, I'd brushed and aired the hangings for Mother and Father's chamber and the bed coverlet that matched them. Mother had worked them herself during the first year of their marriage in a pattern of their interlaced family shields surrounded by tiny hearts, flowers and unicorns. We cleaned the deputy's palace from top to bottom, airing the rooms and scrubbing away the dirt left by the string of deputies who'd occupied the place since Father's removal. Poynings' unorthodox household had been the worst and the dirtiest, for the explanation the palace servants gave for every broken pediment or tile was that the Poynings children had done it. Still, we soon restored the place to cleanliness and order so that that, at least, would be as it had been in Mother's day.

But it wasn't until September 17 that Michael, who'd been sent to give advance warning when Father's ship arrived at the quay, galloped through the nether gate with the news that Father would be at Saint Thomas Court within the hour.

Then was the castle in an uproar. We hurried the children through washings and changings and dressed the baby in her best. Walter laid the table so fast that the trenchers were warm from the speed and orders were shouted for the cooks to bring out the best to be had on short notice, while Walter ran with the best muscatel bottles to the well to cool them in the bucket lowered into the depths of the water. Alice stripped the pleasance for flowers for the table and a great bundle of them—gillyflowers, autumn roses and phlox—to give to Father. Miraculously, we were all dressed and ready in the courtyard except Grandfather, who was too sick but who made Michael stand in his window to report everything to him when the herald arrived.

He was English, of course, since none of our own people had been in England with Father, and he was dressed in livery so new it shone. Apparently, then, Father had so adopted the English ways his people were henceforth to wear livery, I thought, with mingled amusement and dismay. I could scarcely imagine such a condition at Maynooth. But as they filed through the gate I could see that Father had brought a sizable retinue. There were even women among his party. Puzzled, I gazed as they advanced; two plainly dressed girls, obviously servants, rode behind him and the third woman. She was quite a different matter.

She was about my own age or a little younger, small and pretty with delicate English coloring, blue-green eyes and fair, wispy hair escaping her pearled headdress. Her gown was fine and of a fashion obviously new and smart, like those I'd seen in the English court, and of a soft, rosy color that made her glow like a flower beside Father's darker clothing. She seemed excited and chatted animatedly with Father, craning to see us standing together waiting for him.

He jumped from his horse's back and ran forward, shouting our names, laughing, trying to gather us all into his arms at once, then standing back to look at us, taking the baby in expert arms and kissing her exuberantly so that she whimpered and squirmed down from the great stranger, running to the shelter of my skirts.

"Nay, sweeting," I said, "you must not be afraid of your father."

I picked her up and held her in the circle of my arms, and Father, restraining himself, although there were tears in his eyes that his own little one didn't know him, smiled invitingly and held out his arms to her. In a moment she went shyly into them, to everyone's delight.

Then Father turned toward the lady, handing Joannie back to me while he helped her alight from her mount.

"Lady Elizabeth, here they are. My children. Eleanor, Margaret, Elizabeth, Alice, Eustacia and Joan, whom I have only just met. Are they not as fair as I said them?"

"Aye, Gerald, they are indeed," she said, slipping down to stand in the circle of his arms.

My mouth was open, I know, as wide as Eleanor's, and she could have captured an owl in hers.

"Children, darlings," Father was saying, "come here and kiss your new mother. May I present my wife, King Henry's cousin, the Lady Elizabeth Saint John."

I thought the meal would never end.

Everyone, from the serving men to Eleanor, seemed beguiled by the Lady Elizabeth as she sat in Mother's accustomed place beside Father on the dais. To be sure, she'd tactfully taken the place on his left, suspecting, I thought, from the look he'd thrown toward Mother's armchair at the right of the master's, that he had spared a thought to his first wife.

It was the only sign I saw from him that he gave any thought to her.

Obviously, he was much smitten with his Lancastrian wife. He deferred to her and shared a loving cup, watching each sip the dainty lips consumed as if she'd accomplished some astonishing feat to be able to feed herself, indeed. The happy, celebrating tone of the dinner was marred only by his concern for Grandfather, who'd been unable to come to the table, and he'd taken his new wife up to meet Mother's father before sitting down to eat. He was obviously upset by the condition Grandfather was in, but even that didn't dissipate entirely the festive air at the table.

I stared at the two of them in disgust which I could scarcely hide. A scant six months before he'd sobbed out his heartbreak at Mother's death in my arms, swearing he had no desire to go on living without her. Now here he was, cavorting like a boy, for a lass young enough to be his daughter. How inconstant men were! How unfortunate the woman who allowed herself to love one of them. I had thought my wonderful father a knight and faithful lover on a par with Lancelot or Tristan, willing to die for love of his lady. Yet, with my poor mother scarcely cold in her grave, even though she'd died for worry about him, he was gazing into Lady Elizabeth's soft eyes as if the act gave him intense pleasure, Mother obviously forgotten.

Walter, directing the carrying of their baggage upstairs, gave orders to one of the house carls to carry the Lady Elizabeth's to the master's chamber. Before I could stop myself, I gasped out a strained "No."

"Magheen, you forget yourself," Father said sternly, "pray apologize to the Lady Elizabeth."

"She cannot sleep in Mother's bed . . . beneath the coverlet Mother worked with her own hands," I choked. "Forgive me, Father, but take . . . take another room."

Lady Elizabeth stared at me with understanding eyes, which, unaccountably, only made me hate her the more. "She is right, Gerald, I understand how the lass feels. Margaret, where would you like to have my things taken?"

"Back to England," I blurted, then, painfully aware of my own ill-temper and her strained face, jumped up and ran from the hall, followed by my father's angry roar. I didn't stop until I reached my own room and sank down on the bed.

Of course he wouldn't let that pass, and, predictably, in a moment, Father was banging on the door, then pushing it inward without waiting for an invitation to come in.

"That was the most ill-mannered display of rudeness and churlishness I have ever seen," he thundered.

"You couldn't even wait until she was cold," I countered. "Now I understand the matters in England which needed your attention so that you couldn't even come home to see the daughter Mother gave her life to bear for you."

The furious color drained from his face and I saw that I'd hit the mark. It only made me loathe myself. Yet I couldn't apologize. All I could think of was my poor mother's face as she lay dying, his name the last that crossed her lips.

"I . . . I came as soon as the treaty was signed. The . . . my marriage to the Lady Elizabeth was part of it, Magheen," he said in a strained voice.

"Ah, your *sacrifice* in the interest of peace is very great, Father," I said with bitter sarcasm. "No doubt you must steel yourself for the ordeal of lying with her each night."

He darted a lightning slap at my cheek.

"You go too far, girl," he said icily. "I understand your feelings of grief and betrayal. But I cannot allow you to abuse a lady who's done you no harm and, indeed, has given me the will to live again."

I didn't answer him, only turned away so that he'd not see the angry, hurt tears on my face. My father, who never in my memory had ever struck me, had done so now because of his Lancastrian wife. They had cost me dear. My heart ached with the pain I'd endured because of them. Indeed, sometimes I felt I was no longer quite sane for pain and deprivation and loss.

"I am happy for you," I said woodenly. "At least Mother's death served one useful purpose, then. Freeing you to marry this English *child*."

He sighed deeply and dropped down on the coffer at the foot of my bed. "God, Magheen, you're contentious. Never will I understand you. You're a woman now and ought to realize that life is for the living. Surely you understand how dearly I loved your mother. The Lady Elizabeth can take nothing from that. I . . . I will even admit to you that your mother was my true love. My first dear sweetheart. But I have lost her and I'm not the man to live as a monk. Moreover, the children need a mother and she's very kind if you'd but give her a chance. She is pretty and lovable, and that is to my advantage. But had she been seven feet tall, toothless and ugly, I would have had to marry her. It was the king's desire. And you, of all people, ought to know that's the same as a command."

"One you obeyed with alacrity," I said stubbornly.

"There is no use talking to you. Why the hell aren't you with your husband where you belong anyhow?"

"Because we have parted," I snapped miserably. "We do not see eye to eye. Though, now that you're fully restored to the Tudor's favor, he'll not be so afraid of being tarred with a traitor's brush and will likely be coming around."

"Did you ever think he might not want you because of your tongue and not your family association?" he said bluntly.

"Leave me alone, Father," I said angrily, as usual, hiding my hurt behind ill-temper. "I will try to stay out of your way and *hers*. You have seen, of course, that Grandfather is dying. He needs me for the time being. When he's . . . when he is . . . gone, I'll go."

"Where? To Kilkenny? There's a Lancastrian there too."

"I guess that's *my* problem. You needn't worry about it. Go back to your Lancastrian wife."

He sighed again but got up from the coffer and went to the door. "We'll both do what we can to help you, Magheen, but, by Saint Bride, you'll have to change your attitude or the world will devour you."

And with that he was gone, shutting the door quietly behind him.

I lay on my bed mourning. For my mother. For the old, high-hearted, blithely happy, noisy Gerait More, for my own lost youth and unrealized dreams. And for my grandfather, dear and fragile and rapidly slipping away from me too. In a little while I got up and dried my tears and went to him.

As the fall wore on, Father's wife took over more and more of the children's care and the running of Maynooth. I resented this bitterly, although without her I didn't know what we would have done, for Grandfather was melting away before our eyes. The canker grew with alarming rapidity, and soon he could no longer eat anything but the thinnest of gruels, milk and ale. He grew weaker and so thin that his eyes seemed like enormous sapphires sunk into a parchment-covered skull. Nell, Agnes, Elizabeth and I took turns staying with him day and night, for his pain was great and the poppy juice the leech gave him made him foggy and sleepy.

At last, the ever-narrowing passage in his throat would allow the swallowing of nothing but water. Then did his son Thomas, the only other of Mother's family left, and, so, doubly dear to me now, come each day, riding the twenty miles from Kilcullen, to fetch fresh water from the spring on his manor lands, which Grandfather had always declared to be the best in Ireland. The sight of Uncle Thomas, big and silent, his blue eyes awash, striding into Grandfather's room and putting the jugs of water on the cold windowsill, came to be the high point of Grandfather's day. Each small service we did for him brought his thanks and blessing. Once he opened his eyes and smiled at me, his dear old face, once so handsome, ghastly and distorted by the malevolent growth. Painfully he croaked out his words, so that we had to lean over close to understand.

"Magheen, it's . . . occurred to me . . . that . . . all . . . all over the world . . . there are people . . . helping those . . . like me . . . who can't help themselves," he said. "Darling . . . I . . . I . . . was a hell-raiser like all lads . . . in my youth. At the end . . . only the kindness . . . only the . . . love matters. All the rest . . . is nothing."

Soon after that, the only thanks he could give us was a gentle pat on the cheek.

I had never felt such an agony of the spirit.

Watching by Grandfather FitzEustace's deathbed was bad enough. Moreover, I missed Mother's light step and gentle voice every minute of the day. I could not handle this ordeal of Grandfather's illness without her, and yet I had no choice. And, all the while, Father's new wife continued to usurp Mother's home, husband and children. I saw that they were all coming to love her, and I despised them for it. Piers, too, who never came near. How could I ever imagine I loved a man who'd leave me alone with such trouble and pain to bear? I hated him. I hated all the damned Lancastrians, and, when Grandfather was gone, I intended to go far, far away from Ireland. Where, I had no idea, nor how I would earn my bread. Nor had I time to worry about it, with concern for Grandfather's suffering foremost in my mind.

By Saint Nicholas Day, I was praying ceaselessly for his deliverance. He never complained. Indeed, in his few really lucid moments, he tried to smile and speak our names, but his suffering was terrible. When he finally died early on the morning of December 14, I felt a great relief, a sudden lightening of my heart that astonished me. It was as though I'd already gone through the grieving process and could feel only joy that he no longer had to suffer. The odd, dull gratitude persisted through the next day when we buried him at the convent of Minor Friars at Kilcullen, which he and his wife, my Grandmother, had founded.

We went home to Maynooth so that Saint Thomas Court could be cleaned. We would have gone before to spend Christmas but for Grandfather's illness. It was here that Brother Jenicho, our scribe, sought me out with a letter Grandfather had given him for me.

He had, Brother Jenicho explained, made some changes in his will after Father had come back with his Lancastrian wife and had, at that time, written the letter for me. When I saw the familiar, slanting, spidery writing, the grief I'd thought ended engulfed me again. Sick as he was —indeed, the script was wavery and hard to decipher—he had thought to write to me. I broke the wax seal and spread out the single sheet of foolscap.

"Dearest Magheen, child of my heart," it read. The flowery words evoked Grandfather painfully and I could almost see his dear, handsome face, unravaged by the disease, and hear the soft, rapid speech of him. "I have seen how very much you suffer under the same roof as the Lady Elizabeth. I understand it, dearest; after all, it was my beloved Allison whose place she fills now.

"I realize, too, that things are not as they should be between you and Piers. You are both stubborn, no doubt, and striving for your own way. I know as well as anyone that *you* are. But he has not been blameless in this alienation either.

"Therefore, I have insured that you will neither have to live in misery with your father and his wife nor crawl back adjectly to your husband to escape doing so. I, who have filled you full of romantic notions, realize, as you do not, yet, that you would be forced to one of these actions. The only alternative would be a convent, which I can't see you taking. So, though I have left my lands and wealth almost equally between Thomas and your father (You see, sweetheart, I have forgiven him entirely for marrying the Lady Elizabeth. He was constant and true to your mother while she lived, and believe me, even *she* would not expect him to pine away for her now.), one small legacy goes to you. There is a codicil that says, 'To my beloved granddaughter, Margaret Fitzgerald Butler, for her use as long as she desires, irrespective of her marital status, the manor of Newall with all rents and appurtenances thereto. When she no longer needs or wants it, it shall revert to her father, Gerald Fitzgerald, Eighth Earl of Kildare.'

"You see, Magheen, I, who was responsible for your romantic notions, have given you the means to fulfill them. You can be independent as long as you live if you so choose. If Piers has so far come to his senses to realize the treasure he's neglecting, let him come and earn you. Let him woo and win you back to his hearth and home. My dear, wild, high-hearted lass, I could not bear to have the spirit of you beaten down.

"Now pray for me, lass, as I shall for you if it's permitted me. And don't let your pride keep you from seeing the value and goodness of the Lady Elizabeth and from giving your love freely wherever it is needed and wanted. Your Grandfather FitzEustace."

Then did I truly realize my great loss. How I had loved him! I prayed that he and Mother both knew it where they'd gone. Nearly their last thoughts were of those they'd loved. I wanted to be the kind, forebearing, loving girl they both wanted me to be, but I could not forgive those who'd taken all I held dear away from me. I was overwhelmed with gratitude that Grandfather had put in my hands the means to escape an intolerable situation.

The Lady Elizabeth came to see me as I packed to leave. She had never sought me out in my room, and when the timid tap came at the door I thought it was one of the children and called, "Enter."

She glided in gracefully and stood inside the door, smiling gently. Startled, I stared unspeaking at her.

"Lady Margaret," she said softly, "I just . . . well . . . I hope you'll not take offense if I say that I am sorry you are leaving. I want you to know that you are welcome here as far as I'm concerned, always."

Her unselfishness irritated me. "Come, Lady, you can't mean to tell me you *enjoy* having a skeleton at the feast," I drawled.

She flushed but lifted her chin as if determined to have her say. "We have no quarrel that I have been a party to. I . . . I must tell you that your attitude grieves your father, and his happiness is important to me, whatever you may think."

"Oh, I never doubted that. That, at least, you have in common with my dead mother."

"I take nothing from her, Lady Margaret," she said mildly. "Had she still been alive, your father would not have looked my way. But since she is gone, I would give my life to make him as happy as he can be without her. I think that's pretty happy, if he could only stop worrying about you."

"He can stop," I said more reasonably. "It's for the best, Lady. I am going to my own manor and will be within five miles, should you need me. I hope . . . my sisters will come to see me sometimes."

"How can you doubt it? Of course they will. And we'll all pray for you too, that you will finally leave off grieving and come to happiness."

I turned away so that she couldn't see my tears. She might at least have the decency to be a bitch, I thought wryly, so that I could have a good reason to hate her. "Thank you," I choked gracelessly.

"Stay until after Christmas," she said impulsively.

"No, Lady, I have no heart for Christmas at Maynooth," I said sadly. "But, when I've reached Newall safely, I'll send Lionel back in time for spending it with you."

"God go with you, then, Lady Margaret. May the Christ Child ease your heart."

Newall was only a small tower, great hall on the main floor, cellars and guardroom below the hall, master's solar and a small nursery and a storage room above it. Indeed, the lasses who kept the place slept in the village at night, disliking the solitude. The reeve and his wife had a room over the gatehouse, so that when Lionel had returned to Maynooth after escorting me to my new home, I was virtually alone.

There was much to be done to make it a home, I thought ruefully, but destitute as I was of hangings or books or plate, at least it was mine, with lands enough to support it. I would make a life for myself here; I had no need of anyone except myself.

On Christmas Eve the wind-driven snow began to pile up on turrets and windowsills and I pushed the wooden shutters into place, not really keeping the cold at bay. But there were logs and peat in plenty and I built up the fire in the hall, sitting solitary before it, thinking of past years when we'd been happy children at Maynooth. There'd been games and oranges and new clothes. Sweets and toys and Father booming happily above the din. Gone, all gone. And no one of my own to take the place. I should have had a happy home and several babes in the nursery by now. I would grow old and die, all alone here at Newall. Tears slid silently down my cheeks.

"It's what you wanted," I reminded myself wryly.

Even the reeve and his wife had gone off to midnight Mass. But for my own pride, I could have been at Maynooth. But the thought of Father gifting the Lady Elizabeth as he once had Mother, teasing like a small boy for her to open her presents from him early, brought bitter tears to my eyes. I was better off alone.

The knock at the great oak door was as startling as if I'd been on a deserted island. I was suddenly, terrifyingly aware of my vulnerability. But this was to be my life from now on, and I had to take care of myself. So, lifting my chin, I grasped the handle of the heavy poker and went to unbar the door. It swung inward slowly. The light from the fire fell on a solitary figure.

It was Piers.

CHAPTER 8

He was surely a figment of my imagination, I thought, the poker hanging unheeded at my side. So often had I dreamed of him staring down at me, smiling that enigmatic smile of his, that I'd conjured him up to torment me in my isolation and solitude entirely.

The figment of my imagination beat his hat against his flank, scattering snow across the doorsill. "May I come in, Margaret?" it said. "It's colder than the bottom of the channel out here."

I stepped back, too dazed to speak, and put the poker in its usual place near the hearth. He advanced toward the fire, extending his hands to the blaze. He acted as if he'd only just been gone a few moments to see to the weather conditions, perhaps, instead of nearly a year.

"What is it you want?" I said, finally gathering my senses a little.

"I am sorry you have lost your grandfather," he said in the maddening way he had of ignoring my question by making an unrelated statement.

"It was a blessing," I said, "since his suffering was very great toward the end. But how did you know of his death?"

Again he ignored my question entirely.

"They say at Maynooth you were like a staunch cedar they all leaned on through the troubles. That, but for you, things would have been much the worse."

I was pleased that they'd so praised me but only nodded grimly. "I don't think they could have been much worse," I said.

He threw hat and cloak toward the table, not taking his eyes from me.

"You are thin, poor lass, and there's sadness in your eyes."

All at once the sorrow and suffering I'd endured caught up with me and I began to cry, my face contorting, I knew, most unbecomingly. Before I knew it, he had me in his arms. Too startled and overcome to resist, I stood there feeling the comfort of that encircling with confusion and a strange acceptance.

"Oh, Piers, it's been so awful," I sobbed against his chest.

"I know, lass, I know," he said kindly. "And brave you were about it too."

"Oh, why can't you be like this always?"

"Kind, Magheen? Caring about you? Was I not always?"

"When it suits you to be," I sighed, pulling away a little.

"Well, when did it ever not suit me to be, then?"

"After Gerry was taken. When Mother died. Oh, where were you when I needed you?"

"You sent me away, Margaret," he said reasonably. "I am not the man to stay where I'm not wanted."

"And you hadn't sense enough to ignore me? I was so alone. I thought I couldn't do it all. I needed you."

"But you *did* do it all alone, Margaret. You always have. You've never needed anyone."

"What good would it have done me to expect help from you?" I flared. "You were only concerned with saving your own hide with the king. How did you express it? You 'didn't want to be destroyed by the cursed Geraldines,' wasn't it?"

His jaw jutted stubbornly, but his lips remained slightly smiling. "I'll not defend myself to you, Margaret," he said sturdily.

"And now you're back," I continued in spite of myself. I couldn't govern my sharp tongue even though I longed to be back at peace with him, longed to be again in his arms. "I suppose, then, it's because my father is no longer in disgrace and you can associate with us Fitzgeralds without incurring the king's suspicions."

"Think what you want. But *I* didn't leave you; you told me not to come back," he said.

"Then why are you back?"

"You are the most impossible woman I've ever known," he exploded. "Nothing I ever do pleases you. I swallowed my pride to come here, and are you willing to meet me halfway? No, you're off harping about things best forgotten."

"Well, if you don't like my harping, why don't you just leave me alone?"

He was maddeningly silent. Angered at my own ungovernable nature and his impenetrability, I turned away, making a futile sound and gesture. His eyes seemed to soften as I watched him out of the corner of my eye. Yet his silence, his quiet air of reason in the face of my agitation, as ever, drove me on.

"By Saint Bride, you leave me alone to cope with sickness and starvation and death, you are gone, God knows where, for nearly a year, then you show up on my doorstep when I'm finally trying to make a home and life for myself, and I'm supposed to leap into your arms and say, 'Oh, Sir Piers, how happy I am, entirely, to have you home,'" I shouted.

He laughed unexpectedly and exuberantly. "God, Margaret, you sound exactly like Gerait More when you're in a temper," he said.

"Don't talk to me about my father, either. He's turned out to be a bigger Lancastrian than you."

His eyes snapped with laughter. "So your father has feet of clay. How terrible for you, who want everyone to be perfect. I remember in the old days, all I ever heard from you was what a great knight your father was, how well he ruled the Pale, how gallant his Yorkist sentiments, how devotedly he loved your mother . . ."

"Shut up about him loving my mother," I cried, feeling angry tears welling again.

He stared at me for a long moment. At last he shook his head as if in understanding and sympathy. "Ah, that's it; you're thinking him lacking in love and respect to have married so soon."

"It doesn't matter what I think. No one ever cares what I think."

He took me by the shoulders and stared at me earnestly.

"That's not so, Margaret; you're only giving way to self-pity now. I care, as do all who . . . who are concerned with your well-being. You must not be so hard on your father, though. He has need of a home."

"He *had* a home."

"A home needs a woman in it. My home needs you. Don't you think it's time you came back to it?"

"I *am* home. I am happy here," I lied, too stubborn to let him see how his words had moved me.

"Is that why you're crying?" He touched my tears then, put his hands on either side of my face and turned my face so that I had to stare into his eyes. Held so, I knew that he would read the longing in my own. I loved him so much. Why couldn't we be as one? Why could he not be to me as I was to him? As if in answer to my unspoken questions, he drew me smoothly into the circle of his arms. He made of them a warm cocoon from which I wanted never to emerge. Lifting, he gently guided my face into the hollow of his neck, cradling me at rest, then, drawing back with infinite tenderness, covered my lips with his. For a long, blissful moment, there was only content, the quiet, happy sense of being home after a long, weary sojourn. But then, with a sudden, insistent clamoring, our senses seemed to awake as one to a deep, clinging, longing need.

We held each other, kissing with growing fervor. Longing, wanting, and at last, there by the fire, loving. We never cared for aught else until the fire died and the stone

floor grew cold. Then did we go to my bed and slept the
night away in each other's arms.

The dawn making slits of light through the shutter slats
awakened me.

Piers was leaning on his elbow, gazing down at me, a
tender smile on his face.

"You sleep like a child, Magheen, snuffling softly, your
face on your hand," he said.

I stretched and smiled, all the suffering and longing a
faint nightmare, rapidly dissipating in the morning.

"Oh, Piers, I didn't know . . ."

"That you snuffle?"

"That . . . that . . . such . . . oh, that it could be so
sweet," I said, suddenly shy for the first time in my life.

"Was it sweet, then, Magheen?"

"Aye. As sweet as all my longing for you has been
dreadful."

"You've been longing for me?"

"Oh, aye," I said trustingly. "Couldn't you tell?"

"And are you longing now?"

"I think so."

"Then we must needs do something about it."

"Oh, aye," I breathed as he kissed me.

It was some little time before we remembered it was
Christmas.

The following weeks were like some sweet idyll. Although I knew Piers had much to occupy him at Kilkenny,
and indeed he wanted to return there, he stayed with me,
showing little sign of impatience with my hesitancy about
leaving Newall.

"Then, Newall is yours, Margaret?" he'd said as we ate
our Christmas breakfast of oatcakes and ale, for there
was little else in the house, so scant had been my interest
in celebrating the day.

"As long as I want it," I explained.

"I suppose you're about the only woman in Ireland with

unencumbered property of her own," he said after I outlined the terms of Grandfather's bequest. "As long as you
live here, neither I nor your father could touch it nor take
it from you."

I glanced at him sharply. "That's right. My grandfather
wanted me to be free to choose whether I'd stay with my
father or go to you or just live on my own for the rest of
my life."

"You'll come with me now, won't you, Margaret?" He
took my fingertips and kissed them, his eyes inviting me to
remember what had passed between us.

I stared at him silently. So swept away had I been by
the joy of our union that I'd not considered anything so
mundane as property rights. But the fact was that he was
right in pointing out my unique position of being my own
mistress though married, for by law, everything a married
woman might have inherited belonged to her husband.
Grandfather had neatly forestalled this by giving me the
use and revenues of Newall as long as I stayed there and
wanted them but allowing it to revert to Father should I
decide other. I had been so happy with Piers last night
and now, in the winter dawning as we contentedly shared
the simple breakfast.

But it had not always been so. How did I know that
once I surrendered Newall to Father and myself to Piers
he would not revert to his old mocking, superior self? My
heart told me it was not so, but then a chilling voice within
me insisted, What if it is? There would again be nowhere I
truly belonged. I never wanted to feel the insecurity of
these past months after Mother's death.

"I don't know, Piers," I said honestly.

"I seem to remember you telling me you loved me at
one point last night," he said, mockingly tender. "And if so
you do, then don't you want to be with me?"

"I feel as if I'd die if I were ever separated from you
again," I said honestly, thinking with sudden disquiet that
he hadn't said he loved *me* at any point. "But it's a big step
for me. One from which there is no turning back once it's

taken. I . . . oh, Piers, try to understand. I felt so vulnerable . . . so besieged by events that governed me entirely
. . . maybe . . . maybe I'd be sorry later if I agreed to return to Kilkenny."

"It's grander far than this small tower," he said, ill-dis-
guised contempt in the encompassing gesture he made.

"Don't be obtuse, Piers, you know what I mean," I said,
taking his hand. "It isn't what my grandfather intended,
that I should abandon what he gave me so lightly." I
stopped, thinking of the dear letter he'd written. How he
understood what I felt and what I needed. Let Piers earn
me back to his hearth and home, it'd said. And, in spite of
my happiness, I knew he had not. After all, I was a not un-
comely maid, his wife, and my family was once again the
foremost in Ireland, well in favor with the Tudors. It was
only expedient of him to want to resume our marriage
now.

His face was a thundercloud but, chancing to glance up
at me, his expression softened and he smiled.

"You are going to make me crawl, is that it, Magheen?"

"No. I should not like you 'crawling.' I just want to be
assured . . ." I stopped. How could I tell him that I just
wanted to be certain he cared for me? That he *loved* me? I
knew that, should I voice such sentiments to him, he'd
smile cynically and tell me we lived in Ireland and not
Camelot.

He took pity on me. "I understand, lass. No, it's all right,
really I do. Then, perforce, I must let you take your time
deciding you're ready to be my wife and chatelaine of
Kilkenny in very truth."

"Thank you, Piers. I do understand how difficult it is for
you to try to understand my whimsy."

"You want to be wooed and won, then?" he said with
the air of one determined to understand.

I laughed in spite of myself. "I guess you might say
that," I agree. "You make me feel like a moonstruck fool of
a scullery maid, dreaming of a prince on a white horse

bringing her word that she's an empress kidnaped in child-hood and disguised as a servant."

"Why is not life as it is enough for you, Margaret?" he said, suddenly earnest. "You must always be wanting storybook things. Happily ever after."

"Is that so bad? I think I should go mad at all the pain and sorrow in the world if it weren't for my dreams," I said thoughtfully.

"All right, lass. I'll try my best to fill your dreams for you," he said, drawing me to my feet. "Shall we start by a romantic walk through the snow to Mass? After which, perhaps you can think of something even more romantic to do."

And so we went on through January and February.

We had frequent visitors from Maynooth—Nell, who seemed to be coming out of her grief over Calvagh at last and had agreed to let Father treat for another marriage; Elizabeth, who'd been betrothed to Christopher Fleming, Lord Slane, over the holidays; and Alice, who was soon to marry our cousin Conn O'Neill. Father and the Lady Elizabeth didn't come. I was at once hurt and relieved by this, though Piers said they'd come quickly enough if they didn't feel defensive about my attitude toward their marrying so precipitantly. However, Alice eased my conscience unknowingly when she said the Lady Elizabeth was pregnant and ailing. Perhaps that was all that kept them away and not my own unforgiving heart.

I missed my father and the children terribly and longed to be reunited with them, but I had never been good at admitting I was wrong, and my still too-fresh grief at the loss of my mother and grandfather stiffened my prideful tongue all the more.

Then, in March, the suspicions I'd had for days were confirmed when Agnes came to call and, after listening to my symptoms and examining me, declared that I was pregnant too.

"I'm staying with you, lass," she said, tearfully embracing me. "Your dear mother would be spinning in her grave, and that's a true fact, if she knew you were in this way with none to attend you and look after you but that reeve's slatternly wife."

"Oh, Agnes, I'm glad. It'll be good to have someone from home. But won't the Lady Elizabeth be needing you?"

"There are many at Maynooth to look after her, and I know your mother would want me to do for you," she said. Then, throwing me a sidelong look, "What does your husband think about this, Magheen?"

"I haven't told him yet. But now that you're sure I am pregnant, I will."

"You shouldn't be in this dank little tower. 'Tis no place for an expectant mother. You need light and protection from the wind, which, God knows, this place doesn't afford."

"It will soon be summer, Agnes," I said, but in my heart I knew we'd move to Kilkenny. Like many a lass before me, I'd not thought the whispered ecstasy could so readily result in this sudden weight of responsibility. *I* could live on at Newall forever; Piers's child should be at Kilkenny.

The knowledge that I was to have a child, Piers's child, filled me with quiet happiness. Indeed, I was almost ready to relinquish my little tower, whether a child had been on the way or not. Yet, still, a nagging, insubstantial doubt plagued me. When I'd once left Newall for Kilkenny, there could be no turning back. I would be Piers's wife and chatelaine of Kilkenny and the mother of this rare, precious burden I carried. I had savored being my own woman, short though the time. But I loved Piers with all my heart, and Kilkenny would be lovely with the spring bursting out on every hawthorn hedge and the peepers exuberant from the boggy places and the larks bursting their throats with their songs entirely.

If only I were certain he loved me. If only men's promises were worth the believing. If only it was possible for a woman to have the constant, eternal love she was born be-

lieving in. I thought bitterly of Father and his Lancastrian
wife. If he'd truly loved Mother, as he'd always declared
he had, then he would not be so blithe with his new English lass.

But then, perhaps, he was as constant as it was possible
for a man to be. As Grandfather had said, he'd been faithful and true to her while she lived. Certainly I could no
longer hold him up to Piers as an example of undying love.

I seemed to be growing up at last, I thought ruefully.
Piers had said I demanded perfection of those I loved.
Perhaps he was right. Perhaps, though, I began dimly to
perceive, my idea of perfection was unrealistic entirely.
Certainly my husband had given me no reason to fault
him. Though he was not as demonstrative as I could have
wished, neither had he ever failed to be thoughtful and
courteous and kind, treating me like an equal human
being, with wants and needs as important as his.

And that was a rare thing in Ireland, where women, like
as not, were counted among a man's wealth, wives valued
for their profundity and the dowers they brought, daughters for the alliances with neighboring warlords they could
cement.

So, on the whole, I was happy about my pregnancy.

I told him one morning when we'd walked out to watch
the new lambs, a sight we'd agreed was one of the fairest
of the springtime.

"By the rood, Margaret, are you sure?" he said, seizing
my hands, his eyes shining.

"I'm sure. I waited until Agnes confirmed it, for she's
had much experience with such things. She says to expect
the babe near Michaelmas, late in September."

"Then I must have made you pregnant near the very beginning," he said proudly.

I laughed at that. "You men take great pride in such
things, don't you?" I hugged him fondly. It was good to
see him happy and full of himself.

He dropped a kiss on the top of my head. "I suppose we
do," he agreed good-naturedly. "But that isn't the reason

I'm so pleased. There'll certainly be no problem with Uncle Thomas fretting and fretting for me to have an heir now."

I leaned back in the circle of his arms and looked up at him. "Your uncle frets because you'd not an heir?" I said in a strained voice.

Piers was too excited to notice.

"He never stops when I'm in England," he said. "Why, I'd just gotten back shortly after your grandfather died and he'd been huffing about . . . you know that fussy, funny way he has . . . saying perhaps he really ought to consider making one of my grandfather Edmund's descendants through one of my Father's younger brothers heir, since they've proved more prolific . . ."

I slapped his arms away and stomped back, hands on my hips.

"You mean to tell me, Piers Butler, that you sought me out because you wanted to get an heir on me? That you were afraid of being disinherited?" I snapped.

"Partly . . ."

"By Saint Bride, you're a *far* worse rogue than I ever dreamed," I cried, whirling around and stomping away from him. "I might have known there'd be something in it for you."

He fell into step beside me and I was almost running to try to keep ahead of him.

"Just what's wrong with wanting to have a child with my lawful wife?" he demanded.

"You ignored me all through my troubles and woe, and then, when I was weak and lonely and aching for the sound of a human voice, you took advantage of me."

He grinned maddeningly. "Aching you were, but it wasn't the sound of my voice that eased the ache."

"Oh, what a lewd thing to say."

"Don't put on prudish airs with me, Magheen; for, by the rood, well I know you're not."

"I am not a brood mare either, but that seems to be my main value to you."

He burst out laughing, trying to turn me toward him.

"You've more spirit than the finest Arabian mare, lass. God, how your eyes snap sparks at me."

"I wish they could burn you," I said, shrugging away. I wanted to sob out my heartbreak. I'd thought he was beginning to truly care for me. *Me*. But he'd been getting uneasy about his lack of an heir. He'd been in danger of losing his inheritance.

He leaned forward and kissed the tip of my nose, awkwardly, since I would not cooperate. "You never, never bore me, Magheen," he said, laughing.

"I suppose I'm supposed to consider it a compliment that I do not *bore* the great, the superior Piers Butler."

"Why are we fighting? Why do we always end fighting?" he said, exasperated. "I came here, hat in hand, to take you home to Kilkenny. I have even bided here, chafing to be about the administering of my uncle's lands while you made up your mind to resume your duties as my wife and Kilkenny's chatelaine."

"You came to get a child on me," I said stubbornly.

"Which I have done. Now will you stop all this nonsense and come home with me? Don't you think it's time to behave reasonably?"

"Reasonable. Of course. By all means we must behave with reason," I said tiredly. Then, suddenly defeated, I shrugged.

"I'll come to Kilkenny, Piers. After all, what else can I do when I'm bearing Kilkenny's hope? Send word to Father that he can assume possession of this manor, for, once I leave it, it will be his henceforth."

And, turning on my heel, I went into my little tower to pack.

I doubted if my husband could begin to understand what he had cost me.

The Lady Elizabeth bore a child, a boy, in May. They named him Henry but he didn't live to see the roses bloom. I sent a note of condolence back with Lionel, who brought me the news but was unable to go myself, since we'd returned to Kilkenny and my condition didn't allow of such a trip, even for a half-brother's funeral. Lady Elizabeth wrote that, though they grieved for the tiny son they'd lost, she was well and they hoped God would bless them with more children. She said I was much missed at Maynooth. Indeed, her letter was warm and charming, full of news of the children and Father. With gentle tact, she wrote as if we'd always been the best of friends. I realized I had been prickly and an embarrassment to her and longed to be able to apologize, to seek her friendship, but never had it been easy for me to say the tender things in my heart, though the angry ones came out easily enough.

If my own heart was troubled at times by the feeling of entrapment the baby gave me, Ireland at least was at peace.

Perkin Warbeck had attempted to invade England and Ireland the summer before Father returned to Ireland from his imprisonment, and, finding none of the support he'd expected, had sailed away, finally landing at the Scottish king's court. We'd heard that King James had given him a young noblewoman, the Earl of Huntly's daughter, as his wife and they already had a child or two. He'd attempted another invasion of England from Scotland with the Scottish army and a ragtag army of mercenaries and desperadoes he'd gathered from the malcontents of Europe, but had dragged himself back to Scotland in ignominy and defeat. Henry of England was so determined to capture him that he'd been negotiating a marriage between his oldest daughter, Margaret, who was not yet eight, and the lecherous twenty-four-year-old king of Scotland, peace between their two countries, and the handing over of Perkin Warbeck to be part of the marriage treaty. So far, James had evaded the issue, but there seemed little doubt he'd have to agree, for England's might was more than he could comfortably quell, and the princess was, after all, a considerable prize in the marriage game monarchs played. Personally, I couldn't see how

Henry could bear to give his innocent daughter to the amoral James, but of course they'd not marry until she was of age, and by then perhaps he'd have settled down to more decorum.

At least Piers was not like that, I comforted myself.

I wondered what would become of the lad Perkin Warbeck. His end could not but be doleful, that was certain. Too bad he had dragged a woman and children into it. James was expected to expel him, Scottish wife and children and all, momentarily.

Little had been heard of Black James Butler, which was a great blessing to Ireland, for, with the most inclement weather we'd had in many a summer, the people were kept busy digging drainage ditches in their fields, hoping to save some of the crop from rot. Some said he'd gone to Scotland to conspire with Perkin Warbeck, which would have been an abrupt about-face for him entirely after the years of being the Tudors' hound.

Piers spent much of June working in the fields himself, hating to demand the labor days the tenants owed the manor, since they were hard put to save their own harvest. But in July he decided to ride to Dunmore, the rains letting up temporarily, to see how the establishment of Flemish weavers he'd brought over were progressing. It had been a pet project of his, and one I was much interested in as well, to found such industry in Ireland, where fine wool was plentiful as well as linen and the manpower, quick of mind and imagination, to learn the weaving trade.

"Take me with you, Piers," I said as we discussed the trip.

"Are you mad, Margaret? It's thirty-five miles. You are nearly seven months along now, and must see to the well-being of my heir."

I sighed, nodding. Always, it was "the heir, the heir." I knew that he was right; I felt well and had constantly to remind myself that I was an expectant mother. But it was irksome, all the same, biding at Kilkenny like a fat, placid

sow when there were so many things I wanted to do. Not
the least of these was simply being with my husband, for,
unemotional as he was, my love for him seemed only to in-
crease while each day he grew more taciturn, more ab-
sorbed in Kilkenny and the expected heir to the honor of
Ormonde. As if he'd already forgotten my foolish request,
he went on checking a column of figures relating to the
new business, which James White, a tubby, genial little
scribe who helped Piers with the business connected with
running Kilkenny in addition to his duties as vicar of
Ardee, stood by.

"Be ready immediately after Matins, then, Sir James,"
he said at last, closing the account book. "We'll take two
days going, spend a day there, and come back all in the
fourth day."

The little priest nodded and folded the book under his
arm. Then, frowning a little, he seemed to reconsider.
"Don't you think, milord, that perhaps we ought to allow
two days for the return?"

"Nay, when my work is done I want to get home," Piers
said.

I stared at his impassive face. I suddenly remembered
Father heading for Maynooth after the Parliament that
Perkin Warbeck had spoken to. *When my work is done,
I'm like a tired horse heading for the barn and oats. The
Lady Allison will be waiting for me. Her time is nearly
nigh.* The familiar sob died in my throat as I thought of
how life had been then. When we'd reached home, Father
had hugged Mother as if he'd been away a year instead of
a few days.

No doubt Piers would stare at me impassively and say,
"I trust you keep well, Lady." Oh, well, what did it matter? It was time I grew up and stopped expecting him to
behave like Lancelot, I told myself firmly.

The days dragged, sultry with the rain-heavy clouds
that hovered, muttering malevolently of the wet burden
they carried. Piers had told me he'd arrive before dusk on
July 17, and I, restless and lonely for him, sauntered across

the bridge and walked slowly along the southern track, thinking to meet him.

The wood along the way was thick and choked with the undergrowth the heavy rainfalls had fostered. I picked berries to assuage the familiar thirst of my pregnancy, finding many of them rotted but those that were good, sweet and bursting with flavor. The thick air pulsated faintly with distant rumblings of thunder. I glanced up at the sky, willing Piers and the priest to hurry home to shelter from the storm. Indeed, I'd need to get closer to home myself if I were to escape a dousing. I turned back, thinking wryly that I had to take care of Kilkenny's heir.

Behind me I heard the thunder of hooves on the rain-packed road and turned to see Piers and the vicar pounding furiously, lashing their mounts. They nearly ran me down, so precipitate was their ride.

"My lord," I gasped, laughing from the effort of jumping out of the way, "you are, indeed, anxious to be home."

Piers swore and reined in, jumping down in the same motion.

"God's bones, woman, what are you doing out here?"

"I walked to meet you . . ."

"Never mind, get on the horse," he snapped, lifting and pushing me up at the same time. "Ride on, Sir James, get help from the castle."

The priest needed little urging but spurred his mule forward.

"What's amiss?"

"For once in your life just keep your mouth shut and get on . . ."

But there was suddenly no need for explanation. Around the turn of the road came Black James and five men-at-arms, shouting exuberantly, more than a little drunk, I thought, and bearing down on us there in the road. The startled horse reared and headed for Kilkenny, barely missing knocking me sprawling in the road.

Piers took my hand and dashed into the shelter of the woods, pulling me so hard I thought my arm would come loose from the socket, then, getting behind me as if to shield me with his own body, he pushed me along ahead of him.

They couldn't force their horses into the thicket and so dismounted, laughing insanely at the turn their game had taken.

"Head back toward the castle in the undergrowth," Piers hissed. "Our only chance is to outrun them."

I thought we'd little chance of doing that, for they were great long-legged men too excited to notice the briars that caught our skin and scratched. I, on the other hand, was clumsy and heavy, unable to see the roots underfoot that tripped me up. Yet, so desperate were we to escape them, that we eluded them for several long moments before they finally encircled and captured us.

They pinioned Piers between two of them while two more took me between them, half-dragging us to a clearing in the wood. My heart was pumping, my breath coming in short, painful gasps when at last they threw me down on a damp moss bank.

Black James stalked up to Piers, his inky eyes glowing with diabolical glee. "Well met, cousin," he said triumphantly. "How fortuitous that we chanced to meet."

"What are you doing in my demesne lands?" Piers glowered, trying in vain to jerk free of his captors.

"They will soon be *my* lands, dear cousin," Black James chortled.

"You're mad," was the scornful reply. "The king has had his craw full of you."

"The *king* is Richard IV, erstwhile Duke of York, and in exchange for my aid in reaching his rightful place on the throne of England, he's promised to legitimize me and give me these fair lands, which our dear uncle will forfeit for backing the Lancastrian horse."

Piers laughed scornfully. This seemed to anger Sir James. He was far different from the cool tormentor that had come to Maynooth so long ago, now that he was no longer top dog. Indeed, he seemed almost to snarl and, with no warning, struck Piers with vicious force. I screamed as my husband's head reeled back and blood poured from a cut at the corner of his mouth.

"You will not live to see it, Sir Piers, but it will happen nonetheless. Even now we are on our way to Cork to greet His Royal Grace. He'll arrive within the week."

I lunged forward, watching the blood roll down Piers's doublet, determined to staunch it, but Black James pushed me back with his foot. He turned and stared down at me, eyes glowing and baleful.

"So you're carrying his whelp, Lady. Too bad, for you too will have to die; we want no little Lancastrians in Kilkenny. But I have waited long to have you and so I shall. Your husband's child will cause me some inconvenience but . . ." He dropped down beside me and tore at my gown. I screamed and scrambled up and away. I heard another scream, a man's, furious and terrible, and I glanced momentarily toward Piers, who was making that ancient battle cry.

He'd jerked himself free of his two captors and grabbed a spear from the one. He looked ten feet tall and his dark eyes were red with blood while his jaw worked in furious excitement.

"You Goddamned whoreson murdering bastard, stand and face me," he shouted, charging like Thor, or Robin Hood, or . . . or . . . Lancelot.

Sir James turned and drew his battle-ax from his belt and swung it viciously at Piers's advance, but he might as well have tried to stop an army.

Piers drove the spear right through him and pinned him to a tree!

I had thought I was a strong, Irish lass, capable of riding with Red Eva, but the awful sight made me shrink and hide my face. But my heart was quivering with admiration for my husband. Who would have thought my slender, small Piers could have struck such a blow?

The others, drunk though they were, were so appalled at the grim end of their leader that they fell over each other escaping from the wood. Piers ran after them, swinging the battle-ax he'd snatched from the ground where Black James's lifeless fingers had dropped it, but I cried out to him.

"Come back, Piers, I need you," I sobbed.

For, indeed, I did. My labor had begun, just as the rain broke.

Piers lifted me in his arms and struggled back to the roadway, murmuring endearments over and over. "My beautiful, gallant lass. My wild Irish girl. God, Magheen, hold on, sweetheart, I love you. I love you. I'll get you help, darling. Hold on to Piers. I love you, Magheen, you mustn't fret, I'll take care of you."

I stared up at him with naked love. "By Saint Bride, Piers, I'm not fretting, but are you sure *you're* all right?" I said.

He didn't even notice that I was laughing at him.

"Goddamn that filthy, hell-bound rogue, if he's hurt you, I'll kill him . . ."

"Piers, that isn't reasonable, dear, you've *already* killed him." I started to laugh, but another pain caught me and I put my face into the precious curve of his neck and held on instead.

"Oh, Magheen, Magheen, don't die, darling, for, by the rood, I'd not be able to go on," he fretted, reaching the road and staggering toward Kilkenny.

"Father said that too," I said wonderingly, "but he is making a new life now."

"A *new* life, darling, don't you see? Not the dear, old life. But I can't bear to think of that now. You must stay alive. I've not had time to properly love you yet . . ."

"Piers, I am *not* going to die. But, oh, darling, why do you have to wait until you think I am before you say to me what I long to hear?"

But help had come running from Kilkenny now, and I was taken from his weary arms.

He stayed by me throughout the night as my labor continued, praying ceaselessly that it would stop, for we feared it was too soon for our child to survive. But he prayed for me too, me, Magheen. He held my hand and whispered words of love that even I had never dared imagine. I smiled happily in spite of my fear for my babe. Grandfather would be gratified could he but hear what an unsuspected sentimental Irish poet of a man was my Piers.

At dawn of the next day I gave birth to a tiny girl whom we named Sabh for Piers's mother, who'd died at his birth. I didn't see how such a mite could possibly survive, but Agnes made a tiny nest of warmed bricks covered with fine wool and we put her into it, holding her gently each hour long enough to feed her syruped water through a hollow reed and, when my milk began to come in, as much as she could manage in her weakness to suckle. Agnes nodded with cautious approval and ventured that she thought our daughter would live.

"She's your lass, Magheen," Piers said with a grin, "and too damned stubborn to die."

But his teasing, his enigmatic smile did not anger me now, nor ever would again, for I had seen the naked heart of him. I only smiled and took his hand. He was not the wild Irish chieftain, demonstrative and flowery of speech, that I'd dreamed of, but he was a fine, fine man and husband. He would be a devoted, loving father. Like my own.

And suddenly, all my old animosity dropped away, leaving me light, high-hearted and happy as I had not been since the day before Piers had come to Maynooth.

"I've learned my lesson, Piers," I said. "No more expecting my darling ones to be perfect, gods and goddesses. And I'll stop being so stubborn too."

He kissed the end of my nose. "You'd take away the trait I love above all others?" he said surprisingly.

I grabbed him and pulled him to me for a more satisfying kiss. "You know what I mean, darling," I said at last. "I think I've finally grown up."

"Ready to reunite with your father?" he said.

"Aye, and the Lady Elizabeth too. She is a sweet lass,

and mayhap our mother begged Our Lord to send her to Father," I said humbly.

"They're here, Magheen."

"You mean at Kilkenny?"

"Aye. I sent James White to fetch Gerait More and the Guild since they'll need to do something about the pretender if Sir James spoke the truth and they're really coming to Cork," he said. "And the Lady Elizabeth, when she heard the babe had been born and how worried you were of her survival, insisted on coming along to help care for you both."

"I want to see them right away," I said determinedly.

They were not far away. Father seemed bigger and bluffer than ever when he strode into my room, gallantly ushering his Lancastrian wife . . . his *dear* Lancastrian wife.

I would not have had to beg their pardons, for they both saw in my eyes my shame and sorrow to have treated them so badly, but I did anyhow, just before they both grabbed me and hugged and kissed me as if they'd never leave off. Piers brought forward the box, the makeshift nest for our precious bird, smiling proudly as they admired Father's first grandchild, and then did Father grip Piers's hand in friendship and tell him that his Lancastrian wife had told him Piers had spent that year away from me in England, begging the king to believe Gerait More was no traitor. I stared at my father gratefully. His telling me that had been a gentle benediction on my happiness.

I smiled at them all. Piers was right; there was no longer Lancaster and York. There was only friend and family and compatriot for us.

And, I thought, as I gazed into his soft, brown eyes, a dear, gallant and secretly romantic lover.

Author's Note

Little Margaret, "Magheen" Fitzgerald, is fondly remembered yet for her vigor in reclaiming Ireland from the "sluttish Irish" by bringing schools and clean Flemish bedding to Ireland. She was, say the seanachies, "the fairest daughter of Kildare."